By ANDY ELFENBEIN

TALES OF THE FAIRIES OF PINE RAPIDS
The Quyre

Published by DREAMSPINNER PRESS
www.dreamspinnerpress.com

the QUYRE

ANDY ELFENBEIN

DREAMSPINNER PRESS

Published by
DREAMSPINNER PRESS

8219 Woodville Hwy #1245
Woodville, FL 32362 USA
www.dreamspinnerpress.com

This is a work of fiction. Names, characters, places, and incidents either are the product of author imagination or are used fictitiously, and any resemblance to actual persons, living or dead, business establishments, events, or locales is entirely coincidental.

The Quyre
© 2025 Andy Elfenbein

Cover Art
© 2025 Andrei Bat
https://99designs.com/profiles/bandrei
Cover content is for illustrative purposes only and any person depicted on the cover is a model.

Trade Paperback ISBN: 9781641088602
Digital ISBN: 9781641088596
Trade Paperback published November 2025
v. 1.0

For John

ACKNOWLEDGMENTS

I HAVE been so lucky to work with wonderful team at Dreamspinner Press. My deep thanks go to Gus Li and the other editors who read my manuscript with care and intelligence. I also thank my family for being so encouraging. I was lucky to compose part of the manuscript in a beautiful space in San José del Cabo, Mexico. I thank our hosts there for their hospitality. Special gratitude to my husband, John Watkins, for believing in me, and to our cat, Charlotte, for being who she is.

Chapter 1

FOREST, NAKED as a jaybird except for his white socks, started a meeting that would not go as planned.

The man on the screen said, "Hi," and Forest froze, staring.

It was not that the man had a face that answered all Forest's prayers. Maybe late fortyish, sculpted cheekbones, silver hair, a faint salt-and-pepper scruff, a smile that showed teeth just off-white enough not to be fake.

It was not that his body was ripped without being muscle bound. With one look, Forest, himself the owner of a gym, imagined the guy telling stories about weight racks he had known and loved.

And Forest was not staring because the man was rather endowed. (And if you believe that last sentence, fantasy may not be your genre.)

"Calling the meeting to order" is what Forest termed his camming. Since the January departure of Ray, his ghoul of an ex-boyfriend (more on him later), he had had too many of these sessions on his favorite video camming site, LuckoftheDraw.com. On screen, he discovered that everyone looked Undead. If you were going to be hideous no matter what, resistance was futile. But LuckoftheDraw.com notched up the vanity stakes. Only a few souls showed faces, and most hardly showed torsos. It was a parade of the same body part—varied by guys who fell asleep, left the room and forgot the camera was on, never showed up, were behind the wheel on the highway, or were plagued by weird mechanical sounds in the background. They all faced a similar issue, though many ignored it. How do you look impressive enough for someone to pause, but not so contrived as to look desperate? Forest's solution was to buy a fancy chair because everyone knows how much furniture increases sexiness. But, if nothing else, the chair, packed with buttons and levers he had not yet mastered, let him off the hook for not replacing the rest of the furniture now cluttering his apartment like tribbles.

Forest had had a long day at his gym. His highlight was introducing a young trans man to the fitness center. As Forest knew well, the fitness industry had a lot to answer for in its support of toxic gender roles, to say nothing of body images. He was determined that his gym, Forest's Fitness and Pool, would go against the horde of model-thin instructors, ripped men showing off their pecs and six-packs, and yogis in pants that cost more than a week's groceries. The trans man had had bad experiences at other gyms, especially around bathrooms. Forest stressed that all bathrooms at his gym were gender neutral, that the man should feel free to use the men's showers, and that if he detected even the faintest hint of transphobia from anyone, to come straight to Forest, who would handle it.

He hoped that he would see the young man again and prayed that he would like Forest's gym. Every day, Forest had a similar experience of helping people who had worked up the courage, in spite of past bad experiences, to try his gym. That took guts, and Forest did whatever he could to make them welcome. But he had to admit that, while such work was rewarding, it was also tiring, and it left him feeling up to not much more than a mellow evening in front of the camera.

But nothing could have prepared him for this stunning man on screen, who sported a beautiful rich tan—except when he didn't. Even the rise and fall of his nipples as he breathed seemed to alter his skin color, which was always turning into something else. Transfixed, Forest watched as if he were gazing on something scary and forbidden, like RuPaul hosting *The 700 Club*. Was this new cosplay that he had missed? Was it a trend in tattoos? Whatever it was, the guy's skin gave off an aura of greenness without actually being green. It was green-adjacent, green beyond your field of vision, more something you sensed than something you saw. Unsettling, but also exciting in a sort of kinky way. Would "Greenish" now have to be slotted on gay porn sites somewhere between "Gangbangs" and "Gyms?"

"Uh… hi," croaked Forest, sounding as if his voice had died and come back as a zombie. He muffled it so as not to disturb the neighbor, a postmillenarian convinced that Forest's existence proved the coming of the End Times. But what else do you whisper to the Incredible Hulk's lovechild?

An awkward pause.

"I need thy aid," the man said.

Forest's lips smiled, but his eyes darkened. He thought, *And so it ends. He's gonna ask for money and I'm gonna press Next before he's even finished.* Hand raised to the mouse, he was ready to click.

"Would you recommend Mina Flowers's Crispy Chocolate Chunk cookies or think you her Salted Oatmeal ones are superior?"

Forest lifted his hand away from the mouse, once again at a loss.

The man on the screen had spoken of Mina Flowers, whom Forest had accepted as his lord and savior in all things culinary. How did the greenish guy know he loved Flowers and all her works? Was there a clue in the background? Behind him, Forest was aware only of his long, alley-like study, a product of bad seventies architecture. Mothra, his curled-up calico whose wisdom was equaled only by her indifference, lurked in the gloom behind him, but she could provide no clues to the guy on screen. Even more, what was up with how this guy talked? "Thy aid?" "Think you"? Had he spent too much time at the Renaissance Faire? And, most pressing, what was Forest going to say back?

"Uh… I think they're both good."

If there were a prize for dumb answers, he had just won.

"I do too," said the sorta green guy.

"If Mina says to cook them for eight to ten minutes, always choose eight. That way, they won't burn."

"That's sage advice. I abhor burned bottoms… on cookies."

They both grinned a little, and for the first time in weeks, Forest felt connected to someone. No, it was not the funniest joke in the world, but it was authentic, the kind of humor that crops up in ordinary talk. It had been so long that he had almost forgotten what it was like to share a joke.

In the chatbox, a message appeared: "I like what I'm seeing." Forest was amazed. This guy had produced a complete sentence, not the usual "age," "wife home?" or "mmmm." He'd even (oh swoon) used an apostrophe correctly.

And then another sentence, a question this time: "Could I see more?" Only in retrospect did Forest realize that the question appeared without the guy having typed it. Usually, the man on the other end needed at least a minute to send off a blast of eloquence like "hot." But, instead of fretting the syntax, all Forest could think about was that this guy must be a top! So what if he looked like Yoda after a Queer Eye makeover. Bottoms had to make do. A top who could read, spell, and bake cookies was a prize beyond emeralds, and Forest was determined not to mess up.

Years of Pilates and yoga had strengthened Forest's quads, glutes, and hamstrings, and he had no objection to showing off. He slowly turned around to give the camera a better view. Crouched on his desk chair, he saw revealed all the ugly furniture in his long, narrow office: his fake art deco chair, his end table with its marks, scratches, and lines, his floor lamp whose on/off switch was never in the right place, his area rug that never stayed in the right place, and, deep asleep, Mothra. All except Mothra had to go at some point, but Forest never had time.

Another challenge: if you are facing backward to give your camming partner a decent view, just how do you know what they are seeing? With strategically placed mirrors, you might get a sense, but who had time for that? If you turned around to see what they were seeing, your body would twist, thereby wrecking the purpose of looking in the first place.

Forest heard a soft, appreciative "wow." A good sign. It compensated for the basic unfairness that the handsome guy was getting a fun view while Forest was just seeing his long, dingy zoo of an office.

And then it happened. As Forest was moving to provide a better view, his elbow or forearm must have pressed one of the buttons on the chair's arm. The casters reacted as if they had been given a push and rolled away from the camera. Forest wondered why the back wall of his study was getting closer before he realized what was happening. Smiling nervously, he pressed random buttons on the armchair, which responded by traveling backward ever more quickly. He saw his furniture begin to pass by: his filing cabinet, his floor lamp, fitness articles offering contradictory advice on new customers. He also had a tiny "aha" moment when he noticed one of Mina Flowers's cookbooks on the cabinet—that's how the man had known to ask. It was nice of him even to pay so much attention.

But there was no time to overthink because the chair gained speed as it went over the area rug, hurtling away from the camera. So much for camming; Forest had to jump ship. He shifted to put his foot to the ground. Yet his white socks were too slippery to stop a snail, much less office furniture on a rampage. Worse, as his foot touched down and slipped on the area rug, the chair suddenly changed directions (he must have pressed another button) and rolled over his left foot. He yowled in pain—enough to make Mothra open one eye—and threw himself onto the chair, which only hurtled backward even faster as a result.

Forest prayed that something in the chaos would stop him, and something did: his bulky copy of Freeman's *Guide to Nonviolent Communication*. But as he stopped, the chair toppled over, sending him aloft. Like a pizza dough flung high in the air, staying suspended for a moment before falling into the arms of the baker, to the admiration of hungry onlookers, so Forest uprose, eyes wide, heart pounding, limbs flailing, before gravity dragged him into a collision with electrical cords, a gold-and-black lamp, a much-used laptop, a rickety radio, Bluetooth earphones, and leftovers of the Chinese food he had been inhaling to console himself for his break-up. All accompanied by an ear-piercing scream and multiple obscenities.

Lying on a pile of chair, shrimp lo mein, wires, broken glass, USB ports, papers, and his bottle of lube (now oozing over the lo mein debris), he thought he heard "Art thou okay?" from the computer. Despite his pain and embarrassment, Forest was surprised. Most guys would have pressed the Next button a long time ago. Having gone from his sexiest self to the most embarrassing moment of his life, Forest was too humiliated to say anything. Crawling like a wounded crocodile and still naked as a jaybird, he slunk back to the computer, avoiding thinking about how long it would take to clean all this up and just wanting to press Exit. Couldn't the green guy just leave him to his misery? He had just disproved all who thought that camming counted as safer sex.

As he was about to log off, he heard a knock and the voice of Charlie, the building superintendent: "Forest, your neighbor tells me that an earthquake has started in your room. What is happening?" It was not possible for this evening to become worse.

Forest yelled, "I'm battling determined cockroaches" and hoped that lie would be enough. He turned back to the screen. An ad for straight porn popped up (somebody in marketing was not taking their job seriously) and partially covered the green guy. Anyway, it looked like he was turning to go. Preoccupied as Forest was, especially with the pain in his foot, and eager to have it all over, he could not help watching.

What was on the guy's back? A backpack? A jacket? Maybe a scarf? But who wears a scarf while camming, and why hadn't Forest seen it before? But even as Forest was busy overthinking, he knew what he had seen. He just couldn't believe it.

It was a perfectly shaped wing, green as emerald.

CHAPTER 2

RAY'S VOICE assumed an unaccustomed squeak: "You want me to what?" This meeting was not going as planned, in spite of his gorgeous Ferragamo blazer.

"You heard him," growled the one named Fennel, who, with a few small motions of his hands, kept Ray trapped in his chair without actually touching him. Fennel was hardly thirty but, like Mr. Hyde, looked deformed without anyone quite being able to tell why. As he glared, fluorescent lights buzzed in the conference room. On the walls, posters from OfficeMax ("Believe and Succeed!") loomed with sinister intent. At the center of the table, clear plastic cups surrounded an untouched pitcher of water. Fennel broke the silence: "Again. We're paying you for the Product. It needs to be between two and four. Gender does not matter. Candidates are everywhere, so you should have no trouble. And you're going home with a huge downpayment."

Eelie, older than Fennel, sitting upright but looking as if his Xanax had just run out, murmured "Healthy feet." When he arrived at the office this morning, Ray had not expected foot fetishists for clients, but, then again, nothing had prepared him for this meeting. Completely bald, Eelie spoke as if consonants were for peasants. No one heard much that he said, but that never stopped him. Eelie's mention of feet triggered the third one, Garnel (a small, shriveled man), to pipe up with an agitated speech in a guttural language that Ray suspected was not human.

Ray struggled to rise from his chair. He noticed both that his struggles did no good and that his pants were in danger of ripping. His sense of priorities led him to quiet himself fast. His previous meeting that day at Ray's Conflict Resolution had been business as usual: three executive assistants complaining about their boss and each other. Just as everyone expected gay men to be hairdressers and airline stewards, even more believed them to be brilliant conflict negotiators. Ray's one-man operation was thriving, and he had a reputation as a "compassionate communicator," as noted in one of his numerous glowing Google reviews. Forest had told Ray that it was probably a mistake to have written all those Google reviews himself, but Ray had brushed this off along with everything else Forest said.

To those who knew Ray well, conflict negotiation did not seem a natural fit for someone more interested in clothes than people. But he succeeded through his mastery of five facial expressions:

"Interested, but not in a creepy way"

"All your life you have waited for someone to understand you as I do now"

"I'm shocked into silence"

"My heart is breaking into a million tiny pieces" and

"No one could ever get tired of listening to you"

Ray had practiced his expressions in front of his mirror for months until he could assume each with the earnestness of an actor about to meet a messy death in a low-budget slasher.

In a typical meeting, like the earlier ones this morning, Ray cycled through his expressions at about thirty seconds per face. These, plus a smattering of "mmmms," "uh-huhs," and "I sees" cost $500/hour, not including deductibles. His office was a simple one because imposing premises scared away his typical clients. His compassion shone more brightly because the steps to his office were treacherous, the carpet worn, and the retro grunge grungy.

But Fennel, Eelie, and Garnel were not typical. Dressed in green robes, they looked like an eco-cult, an impression furthered by their collective name, which they explained was the "Fae Quyre" (Fennel made sure to spell it several times and stressed that it rhymed with "wire"). At the beginning of the meeting, Fennel had announced, "We're about to offer you three million dollars." It took Ray several minutes to understand what he thought he had heard.

"Wait a minute—what?" he asked. In answer, Eelie held a cup of water upside down over the water jug. Like a miniature Old Faithful, water shot straight up into the cup, which Eelie then deftly inverted. Ray's eyes widened. It hit him that his five expressions were not going to be as helpful as they usually were. Continuing as if nothing had happened, Eelie murmured, "So much depends on the history. I've collected important files for decades." (Several overstuffed legal-size Pendaflexes bulged out of his bag.) "I won't waste your time now, but it all began about twenty years ago when, at a luncheon I had organized at the summer estate, someone recommended the 7th floor of the Paramount Building. I was so surprised. I had never considered the Paramount. It had hardly been touched since the Depression and was packed with so much junk."

"I'm sorry, but I'm not following," Ray interrupted. "I'm a conflict resolution specialist. Is there a conflict that you need help with?" Eelie winced when Ray spoke but otherwise left Ray's question unanswered. Silence filled the room.

At last, Fennel spoke up. "We need a Product for the Rite."

"A what?"

"We are performing the Rite in the renovated 7th floor of the Paramount Building in a few weeks, and we need the Product," said Fennel.

Eelie added, "To help you, I've brought a box of quarto-sized pamphlets about the renovation and how important I was to it. I'll leave them for you to distribute."

When Ray heard "Rite," he just assumed that the trio were Republicans, but they seemed to want something more specific. He asked, "What do you mean by 'Product'?"

Fennel launched a long speech about different ways one could define "product" and what the implications of each might be when Garnel, switching to English, interrupted with unexpected directness: "A young child." At that, Ray squeezed his plastic cup so hard that the ice cubes flew out of it.

"No way."

Silence.

"You've got to be kidding."

"The Quyre never jests," murmured Eelie.

Ray just sat there, expecting something more from Fennel or one of the others. When nothing was forthcoming, he put down the iPad on which he had been taking notes, dumped it in his briefcase, and got up to leave.

"Hold it just a second. We've seen your bank balance. You can't afford to turn us down." (Ray felt himself breaking out into cold sweats, almost as bad as the time Forest spilled Riptide Rush Gatorade on his 1000 Thread Count Sateen sheets). "Just grab some kid, give it to us, and you're three million dollars richer. It's simple. Given that you have creditors baying for your blood and the repo people stalking your car and apartment, you are not in a position to refuse."

And this led to Ray's squeaky "You want me to what?" with which this chapter started, along with his discovery that Fennel had powerful weapons of persuasion, such as gluing Ray's pants to his chair.

Throwing himself back, Ray took out his phone to dial 9-1-1. Fennel smiled. Eelie and Garnel smiled also. "I suspect you're not as alarmed as you want us to believe you are," said Fennel, as Ray's phone leaped out of his hands to smack into the water pitcher. "That money must sound good to you right now."

Ray sighed in frustration as he stared at the three of them. "Why me? If you're so eager, do it yourself."

"We read your Google reviews," Garnel added. "Each more glowing than the next. As soon as we saw them, we knew that you were the man for the job. We could have gotten any brute, but we needed someone who could communicate. Compassionately. And someone so broke that they'd do anything."

Fennel cut in: "You wouldn't want us to think those reviews were lies, would you? For a skilled communicator like yourself, obtaining the Product should be nothing. Given the state of your bank balance, you don't have great options."

Eelie mumbled something that sounded like, "We've cleared your calendar for the next month." How did the Quyre know Ray's clients? How had they contacted them? What had they said?

"But why aren't you doing all this yourself?"

Garnel said, "We can't touch the Product until the key moment, or the Rite is invalid." And with this, he swept up the ice cubes from Ray's cup that were now melting on the table and swallowed them in a resounding gulp. Although he couldn't explain why, this gesture frightened Ray more than anything else that had happened.

"And so I have to find some kid?"

The Quyre's suddenly hostile stares were boring holes in his skull. Suddenly realizing, Ray corrected himself: "I mean… a Product."

Fennel smiled. "You're at rock bottom financially; you have nothing else to do; since you broke up with Forest, you have nobody in your life—"

How do they know about Forest? Ray thought.

"—and you're a great communicator. You'll be paid and run no risk of detection. No-brainer."

Ray pondered while Garnel chattered amiably. "It's easy for people to get the wrong idea about the Rite—especially with all the blood—but you won't have to see any of that."

Standing to go, Fennel said conclusively, "We need the Product in about two weeks. We expect you to start working now." As the Quyre all stood, they reminded Ray once again of monks at an eco-friendly mass.

Ray's mind began to spin. Even as his mind refused their demands, some part of him was already planning where he would find a child. A school? A children's hospital? A church? How would he get it without anyone noticing? And would he be expected to care for it until the Quyre came for it? And just when would he see the money he had been promised? So far, he had no proof that the Quyre could pay him anything at all. He roused himself from his trance and said, "You mentioned a downpayment."

Fennel reached into his robe, took out a sack with an impressive wad of cash, and tossed it on the table as if he enjoyed how hungrily Ray looked at the money. Eelie said, "Once you've taken it, you're ours." It took Ray a second to register that, even though he had heard Eelie's voice, Eelie had not actually said anything. Evidently, being on the Quyre's payroll involved some sort of weird telepathy, and their voices filled his head, so that he could not distinguish exactly who was saying what:

"We didn't want just any thug to obtain the Product. We needed someone respectable."

"A conflict resolution officer is perfect. There will be conflict, and you can resolve it."

"No one will ever suspect a white gay guy."

"You have a month, you get paid well, and then you won't see us again. What's not to like?"

"We're going to enjoy watching to see how you arrange it."

"Parents these days are so overwhelmed that they'll never notice the child is missing."

"As it says on your wall, 'Believe and Succeed!'"

CHAPTER 3

IN THE cold February morning, Forest still had a small limp as he walked into Pine Country Coffee, where he usually bought coffee before his day at his gym. In movies, a jump cut followed disaster. You never had to watch the cleanup—the broken glass, fragmented furniture, the sad "For Sanitation Only" signs, cuts, bruises, and sprains that took longer than you wanted for them to heal. For many days following Forest's mashup of camming and climactic scenes of *Titanic*, he would put his ear to the floor to spy the tiniest bits of glass. It would be days before his study dragged itself out of "aftermath of prison riot" to "messy but livable."

Forest had begun that morning with a thirty-minute Mothra yoga session. Forest's refrigerator was covered with pictures both of Mothra the cat and her namesake. He had memorized Yuji Koseki's immortal Mothra song and could even do a good imitation of the choreography, and he had found a version of the Mothra song perfect for his yoga workouts. Forest also used it as his standard lullaby for the cat. As for Mothra herself, it is inconceivable to her that this book could have reached a third chapter without introducing her at greater length, since who would want to read about anyone else? But even Mothra concedes that on the morning in question, Forest, despite whatever had happened last night, attended to her levee, complete with reliable feeding and brushing as well as obligatory yoga session.

Although Mothra did not talk, Forest would have been the loneliest man ever if he could not imagine her responses to him. When his relationship with Ray was falling apart—soon after it began—Mothra had listened to Forest griping for hours. Through it all, she maintained perfect feline indifference. During yoga, Forest imagined long lectures from her about the inferiority of human to cat yoga, in which all asanas had been renamed for felines (Cat and Cow were Cat and Other Cat, Warriors 1, 2, and 3 were Alleycats 1, 2, and 3, references to dogs had been purged, and those wanting to push their edge could perfect Hairball, Reverse Hairball, and, for the ambitious, Exalted Hairball).

Despite Mothra, Forest brooded on having made a fool of himself the night before. The green guy on camera had seen more of him than anyone except his colonoscopist. If that man had had any decency, he would have shut off his screen as soon as he saw that Forest was in trouble. But he had stayed on until Forest, hands slippery with lube and ego crushed with humiliation, shut everything down. He had even had the nerve to ask, "Are you okay? Is there anything I can do to help?" Forest was furious. How dare he offer help? Forest fumed.

Pine Country Coffee, decorated with fake wooden mini-cabins, skis, moose, and snow, featured mediocre coffee but excellent proximity to Forest's apartment. Today, a hipster in front of Forest needed every item on the menu explained to them—sweetener options, calorie count, containers, source of coffee beans, kind of grind—as if they had never tasted coffee, much less bought it. Forest stood patiently, aching from the bruises of the night before. Brett, the usual barista, would never have put up with such nonsense. Where was she today? But the loser behind the counter ended up giving Mr. Hipster a TED Talk on cappuccino. Forest saw the minutes ticking by until he had to be at the gym.

It was his turn at last, and he was announcing his usual order (skim mocha, no whip) when he heard a loud, brassy voice cut in front of him with "Double espresso."

The barista repeated "Double espresso——anything else?"

Forest froze. He thought he heard someone say, "I think he was next in line," and Forest, bolstered by a tiny bit of sympathy and feeling his bruises, made the mistake of saying, "I think I was right here." But his tiny protest earned him a stare of infinite disdain from the barista. Humiliated, Forest shrank back, coffeeless, and made his way to the water dispenser with the minuscule plastic cups, the refuge of the hopeless. He felt so defeated that he half expected the water to miss the cup entirely or for the cup to collapse when it was half full.

Clutching his water, Forest faced the ultimate challenge: finding a place to sit. As usual, people occupied every good seat, none of them going anywhere. Forest slunk to one of the high-backed chairs facing the window, in the lineup he had nicknamed Incel Row. He climbed up and squinted as the morning sun poured through the floor-to-ceiling glass. Feeling like a specimen under a microscope, he would gulp down his water, check his phone messages, and move on.

"Well, at least thou art clothed," Forest heard a voice say. He couldn't believe that someone was talking to him, but, since he was the only one on Incel Row, the words were unlikely to be meant for anyone else.

He answered, "Well, they're usually on, unless someone asks nicely to take them off." Forest heard the voice chuckling at his response. Forest tried to look in the window in front of him to catch the reflection of the voice's source, but the brightness of the sun made it impossible to see anything. He would have to take a deep breath, turn his head, and actually make conversation. What he saw: early fifties, silver hair, square jaw, green eyes, nice smile. And Forest, as a professional gym employee, knew from the cut of this guy's shirt that he took care of himself. Somehow, his trepidation faded as his look started crossing into a stare. He was aware that the other guy was asking him a question, but Forest was so busy scoping that he hardly heard anything.

"Let's say that I'm concerned about how stable thou mightst be in thy chair right now." Suddenly Forest realized who the man was. In a two-pronged assault, he spilled the rest of his water so that most of it got onto the man and what he did not spill, he spat out in surprise, also on the man. He stared in panic. "I'm so sorry. Let me get some napkins!" Repeating every apology he could think of, Forest rushed to the counter and dared the Gorgon eye of the barista while he grabbed as many minuscule coffee-shop napkins as he could and ran back to mop up the floor, while offering a wad of napkins to the green (sorta) guy from last night.

Forest had seized too many napkins in the hope that, the longer he took to mop, the longer he could postpone what would be an embarrassing conversation. After one of the hottest men he had ever seen had watched him make a colossal fool of himself, he had poured water on top of him and, even worse, spit on him. It was like a BDSM encounter gone awry. Gently, the guy bent down and put his hand on Forest's arm (Forest's heart pounded hard) and said, "I think thou hast cleaned it all. Thanks for the napkins."

Clambering to his feet, Forest tried to think of a sparkling retort and came up with "Okay," plus a vacant stare.

"I have a table with some friends. Come and sit with us."

"Are you sure they're safe with me? I might spit on them too. But seriously, I can stay only for a few minutes. I have to get to work."

"Just a few minutes. And it means a lot to me to see that thou art okay. I was worried last night."

Even as his words made Forest relive all his humiliation, he knew that most gay men would be making merciless fun of him at this point, whereas this guy had been nothing but kind.

By this point, they had come to the table, where the man, who introduced himself as Grant, showed Forest to his friends, Tren and JX. Tren looked like the love child of a toothpick and roll of dental floss and spoke as if consonants were good friends. JX was as broad and generous as Tren was compact, and appeared as if "genderqueer" had been invented for them. None of the three were white, but they weren't obviously anything else either. And in ways that Forest could not articulate, he felt himself relaxing around a bunch of guys who did not pretend to be straight. It helped that Tren and JX were talking in a language that Forest did not know. Those who did not speak English for some reason always put Forest at his ease.

Even as Forest enjoyed getting to know them, a voice at the back of his mind couldn't help wondering: Did Grant's friends also share Grant's greenish propensities? Did they know about Grant? What about the wing thing? And Grant's Renaissance Fairie talk? But Forest's questions would have to wait because no one could get much of a word in next to JX's chatter tsunami: "Oh, Forest, has Grant been talking about you! How cute you are, what a nice body you have, how funny you are, how you're just his type. Can you believe that he had us stake out this coffee shop all morning just in case Mr. Head Over Heels might show up? I mean, we had no way of knowing if you would show up at all, but Grant insisted. And here you are! By the way, don't freak out about his thees and thous. We're trying to get him to sound more like he lives in the twenty-first century because most men can't handle how he talks. His ex said, 'I'm not going to keep living with a man who talks as if he was beheaded by Henry VIII.' Can you believe that some people think he's a Quaker?" followed by a long account of Friends whom JX had known and loved.

This was a lot to take in, but Forest just blurted out, "Wait a minute. How did you even know to look for me here?"

Tren emitted, "Coffee mug."

Looking clueless, Forest repeated Tren's words.

"Where to find you," said Tren, as if trying to win a bet over who could use the fewest words. After thinking about what Tren had said, Forest realized that Grant must have seen his mug from Pine Country Coffee behind him. Indeed, it had gone tumbling during his reenactment of *Titanic*, pushed over by Mothra's acrobatics, and he had meant to replace it this morning until the barista had flattened him. But Grant must have had good eyes to have seen this mug. It was far in the background during the camming session. Did superman vision accompany green skin and wings?

At this moment, a clutch of little girls invaded the coffee shop. They looked like they were part of a birthday party, since they were all dressed as fairies. The visit was presumably for the moms to get some coffee to sustain them through what promised to be a grueling morning of fairy supervision. Forest's gym occasionally arranged birthday parties for young children, so he had seen such groups before and knew just how cutthroat little girl fairy competition could be. What surprised him was the reactions of Grant, Tren, and JX. They all fell silent and had grim looks on their faces. They seemed more than just annoyed by the little girls. Although they did not say anything, the vibe they gave off was one of being deeply offended. For some reason, little Tinkerbells caused an irritation so profound that they could not even speak it.

Trying to lighten the mood, Forest used his usual strategy in such cases, which was to let himself look ridiculous. Since Tren and JX had heard plenty about last night from Grant, he did not have to work hard. Tren and JX teased Forest just the right amount (lots of "bottoms up" toasts with their coffee) but spent most of their time stressing how taken Grant had been with him. They sounded like two yentas making a pitch. Grant was handsome, no longer young, but not ancient, and so deserved a nice guy who could make him happy. Forest enjoyed hearing about Grant but felt as if they were both coming on a little strong. After all, if Grant were interested, he could make his own case.

Instead, Forest decided to change the topic: "It seems like you guys know a lot—probably too much—about me. Tell me about yourselves."

JX piped up, "I'm so glad you asked. Grant here is the town's most glam navigator. He teaches everyone else how to do it, and no one would think for a second to use anyone else. Tren calls himself a hacker, but that sounds so flat to me. I'm trying to convince him that 'security specialist' would be much more employable. For me, documents, documents, documents. I am an archivist. Give me a collection of moldering old paper and I'm in heaven. They're like a huge jigsaw, and I get to put the pieces together."

"Do you work with a particular archive?" asked Forest.

"Oh, yes—" said JX enthusiastically, before Grant interrupted, "I think not that Forest needs to know that right now."

JX stared back at him in shock. Tren stared in front of him, giving no clues.

"You mean he doesn't know?" asked JX.

"Know what?" asked Forest.

Another awkward silence.

"Know what?" Forest repeated. A thought struck him. "Are you pos?" Grant shook his head.

"Married?" said Forest.

This produced a smile from Grant, a roar of laughter from JX, and even a thin grimace from Tren.

"I'm going to follow thy lead and change the subject," said Grant. "Thou workest in a gym. Dost thou teach classes?"

"I want to know what you're not telling me, but yes, I own a neighborhood gym, nothing fancy. We have a nice pool, which most gyms don't have because they're such a pain to maintain. If you or any friends of yours ever want to drop by, please do. I'd love to give you all a month's free membership...."

"Ooooooh—a pool!" said JX. "That would be perfect, especially if there's a high ceiling. It would be a great place to practice my—"

"Forest, I know the gym awaits. Wouldst trust me with a quick word in private before thou takest off?"

"Well, sure, if you can find any place in a packed coffeehouse at peak hours." Grant indicated Forest's former chair on Incel Row, which remained unoccupied. They both walked over to it.

Nervous, Forest chattered, "I'm still so embarrassed about last night. If it had been recorded, I might have gotten a viral TikTok out of it, but I wish I had made a better impression."

Grant said, "First, thou mad'st a wonderful impression: never will I forget. Second, before thou runnest off to work, lend me thy phone for a second?"

Hoping that Grant would enter his contact information, Forest handed over his worn iPhone 9, and Grant held it for just a second, as if thinking about his next move. But he just handed the phone back to Forest after having done nothing more than look at it.

"That's all?" asked Forest with disappointment.

Grant said softly, "Trust me. Just check thy phone. Have a great day at thy gym, and I hope to see thee again soon."

When Forest left Pine Country Coffee, he was a different man than he had been only a few minutes before.

CHAPTER 4

THE WORDS echoed in Ray's memory:

"We can't process the cruise to Puerto Vallarta because your card has been declined. It's at the limit. Do you have another card you can use?"

"I'm sorry, but we're not able to make a down payment on your Kawasaki because your card will not go through."

"Much as I'd like to help you buy those Armani sneakers, I will need a working credit card for the transaction."

And then, rock bottom:

"Um… this is UberEATS. We can't get you that ninety-nine-cent Taco Bell special because your card doesn't work."

Ray went into shock. Life without credit cards: it was like being stranded in some prehistoric nowhere, like *Gilligan's Island* (with no Professor to unbutton in his imagination). Would he become a sad person who lived on a budget? He suddenly saw his impoverished future—sleeping in his car, wearing clothes from Goodwill, showing up in a documentary that only guilty liberals would watch. His eyes overflowed with self-pity.

The Quyre had been right about finances because Ray was deeper in debt than a Classics major with a mortgage. He could have asked his parents to bail him out. He could also have chosen to wear clothes from T. J. Maxx or even consignment shops. But he would rather have walked naked in front of Saks than to lower what he considered to be his standards. There were depths beneath which he would not stoop.

Earlier, after the Quyre left his office, Ray had returned to his high-end condo and did what anyone would do in his situation: nothing. What had happened in the office was so strange that he had to ponder it, aided by his luxury coffee grinder, an expensive Syrah, and a lavender mink bathrobe for special occasions. The next day, he started out by acting as if the whole meeting had not happened. He went to his office, ready to meet with clients and put his five expressions to work. It was not conceivable that the planet could continue turning without his deft "hmmm" and doleful "that's the saddest thing I ever heard." Having experienced them, no one would want to live without them.

But the Quyre had been as good as their word. Ray's calendar had been cleared. His office remained as empty as a theater screening Tarkovsky. He had the bad idea of calling his regular clients. He found himself listening to verbal vomit, usually to explain a sudden upsurge of work/diarrhea/visiting cousins/housing collapse. With a sharp pang, Ray realized that he was not being paid for these calls. To Ray, listening to other people talk for free was equivalent to undergoing every torture scene in *Game of Thrones* at the same time. On his Google Calendar, the blocks for each day, once full of "7 more" or "10 more" markers, were now white shells.

Back home, eager for distraction, he turned to his favorite BoysinBondage.com videos, but just when the muscled policeman was at last getting out the ropes and handcuffs, the computer screen blanked. Lights flashed, electric snow was everywhere, the Blue Screen of Death flashed off and on, and the Quyre's faces appeared, complete with thin-lipped smiles and mutters of disapproval. Ray pressed the X at the top of the screen. Nothing happened. He flattened the picture: nothing. He pressed the computer Off button: nada. He stretched his leg to the power strip and smashed the on/off switch with his foot. But the Quyre, especially Eelie, were still eyeing him coldly from the screen, saying nothing but watching every move. He was not actually frozen to his chair but felt as powerless as if he were. For some reason, Fennel fixed his eyes just beyond where Ray was, as if he were watching something in the background. In time, their faces faded imperceptibly. They had said nothing, but Ray had gotten the message.

In days since the meeting, Ray had almost brought himself to touch the Quyre's money, now sequestered in a green bag on his dining table of flamed mahogany. With their cash, he could restore his balance, pay off his credit cards, go to Puerta Vallarta, get more credit cards, avoid appearing in the sad documentary…. Forest, who guarded money like a gnome with a hoard, used to suggest that Ray might live less like a Central American dictator, but such was the life that Ray loved. Even after his father had been jailed for a bit of insider trading (evidently, no email is gone forever), his mother had maintained the family in sub-baronial splendor. But after her death last year, money had evaporated, while his need for Lamborghinis and Prada had not. But his consulting business, successful as it was, was not quite enough. He had ancien régime tastes on a Walmart budget.

And so the money sat on the mahogany, squatting like a toad. It would solve so many problems for him….

"But I don't know any babies," he whispered to himself as he got closer to the money.

"Um… it's not as if they're hard to find," said a rustling voice that no longer belonged to the Quyre but seemed to emanate from within the bag, from the money itself.

Ray should have been used to such weirdness by now. After the Quyre, anything was possible. But irritation followed his initial surprise. Had he really been reduced to talking to a heap of bills? "I've had all I can take," he muttered to himself.

"Oh, I think there's a lot more right here that you can take," rustled the strange money voice. "You heard the saying 'Money talks'?" A kooky laugh followed, as if bills were crumpling against each other to produce a snicker.

Ray glared, silent.

"I know you're listening. When money talks, people listen—especially with the help of Fennel's magic." More kooky laughter. "The Quyre cannot obtain the baby—oops, the Product—directly or the Rite is invalid. But given the state of your finances, you look persuadable. Money is supposed to be good for change." This last produced a particularly bizarre guffaw of bills and even coins rattling away.

Ray remained silent. The money rustled but said nothing.

Staring at the floor, feeling trapped, Ray whispered what he actually thought: "What happens when I'm caught?"

"That's what you're worried about? That's nothing. The Quyre will get you out."

"Won't this end badly for the kid?"

"OMG. Is this an actual crisis of conscience? From you?"

"First time for everything."

"By all means, take a half a second to enjoy your first and probably last dark night of the soul."

Awkward silence.

The money continued, "Think of it this way. Imagine a time when some brat annoyed you. This is revenge."

Seeing no reason to answer, Ray just stared. Another pause, and the money had a new strategy: "Imagine you are on a long flight. Even in first class, you are cramped. Your feet are swollen, and your legs hurt in unfamiliar ways. You have choked down food that could double as microwaved insulation. You figure out the buttons to tilt back your chair, put on your Bose noise-canceling headphones, and pray for sleep. And at that moment… some quote-unquote adorable toddler starts shrieking at the top of its lungs and continues for hours. The parents shrug and tell you the behavior is age appropriate."

Ray's face darkened as bad memories came surging back.

"You want the noise to stop—who wouldn't? And does it?" Ray shook his head no. "It goes on and on and on. All these months later, you can feel how angry you were, how angry you still are. Use it."

Ray remembered a flight to Sydney on which the baby next to him had screamed, ear piercingly, for twenty-four nonstop hours. His trip to Buenos Aires on which two kids had run up and down the aisles for hours on end dressed as Mutant Ninja Turtles. The toddler who had vomited on his Paul Smith blazer. Toddlers had been responsible for unspeakable hours of high-altitude misery. The more he thought, the more he realized that revenge was succeeding where seduction failed. A (brief) dark night of the soul was succeeded by a sunny morning of profitable vengeance. He'd get the Product not just for himself but for legions of toddler-tormented Platinum Elite travelers. How they had suffered! And had anyone sympathized? One child, more or less, would be a small exchange for the horror and the indifference. Even better, he'd be paid, maybe enough to charter his own kid-free flights.

Almost before Ray realized it, the die was cast. With those images fresh in his mind, he picked up the bag and counted the money. It felt crisp in his hands and had the distinctive mustiness of real cash. As soon as he touched it, the voice ceased. Its work was done. It had been so long since Ray had seen so much cash—or, indeed, any cash at all since his world was credit cards. He realized that he would have to deposit all this cash in a bank for it to be worth much to him. But hadn't he read that depositing so much cash at once raised alarms? His clients usually paid him through Zelle, Venmo, or PayPal, and, with increasing rareness, checks, so cash might seem strange. Maybe if he deposited just a bit at a time….

To his surprise, Ray found himself missing Forest at this moment. He would have liked to have had him as a sounding board—not that he would listen to Forest, but at least he would have had an excuse to hear his own voice. He had no idea how to begin. He knew that gay men could adopt babies, but doing so would take forever. Adoption workers would invade his apartment, and he would have to talk to them without being paid. What about snatching a brat from the park? But he sensed that young mothers in his neighborhood hovered over children like spiders over their prey. The likelihood of a clean grab was low. Look what happened to the burglars in *Home Alone*.

Maybe schools? But the Quyre wanted a young kid, a preschooler. Were there preschools in the neighborhood, where, with luck, he might manage it? Ray planned, considered, evaluated, and did nothing. He took the Quyre's money and spent it with a speed that amazed even him, but, after two weeks, was no closer to obtaining a Product than he had been at the beginning. Would it be enough just to try? The Quyre couldn't criticize him too much if he was trying, right?

CHAPTER 5

FOREST COULD not wait to see what Grant had sent him, but when the moment came to look at his phone, he froze. He couldn't bear to look. What if he didn't like what Grant had sent? What if Grant was so amazing that he could never want Forest? What if Grant's green color was a serious illness and Forest would be in one more gay version of *Love Story*? What if…. After having a panic attack over a message he had not read, Forest put on his happy face and walked into his gym, Forest's Fitness and Pool.

It had started as Rowan's Fitness and Pool, the pet project of his mentor, Rowan, who taught Forest everything he knew about how not to run a gym. Don't focus on beautiful people (they dump you faster than a Grindr date); have classes at all times (never know what fits the schedule); equipment matters less than good instructors (fitness barely needs equipment, but it needs a good leader). Rowan had built the gym before fitness was hot and had had the foresight to include a large pool. In an age when boutique gyms and pricey Pilates studios were devouring everyone, the pool was Forest's trump card. More than once, dollars from kids' swimming lessons had kept his gym solvent, and Forest, in addition to teaching swimming, was a fierce water exercise instructor as well, though he taught anything that would be likely to bring in participants, from Zumba to spinning.

"Um… hi, Forest… there's somebody here to see you? I put him in your office?" said Caroline, the front desk monitor who ended all her sentences with a question mark.

"You what?" asked Forest.

"Put him in your office? He wants to talk to you?"

So the staff was now putting strangers in his office? How could he address this at the next staff meeting? But he'd worry about that later. Now he was fretting the crisis of the week: how to keep the pool open given an absence of lifeguards. He had had to furlough them during the pandemic, and about half had come back. That meant that his big money-maker, the pool, closed for too many hours during the week because he had no one to staff it. Forest had fantasies about kidnapping dolphins and octopi—they were smart, weren't they?—and training them. Although movies treated lifeguarding as the job for attractive airheads, it required training, continuing education, and intelligence. Forest needed to find good lifeguards and soon.

When he came to his office, Forest saw that someone was indeed there, as Caroline had warned, a muscly twentysomething blond wearing a tank top and shorts that left little to the imagination. He flashed Forest a toothy smile, extended his hand, and said in a plummy voice, "Hi, dude. I'm Grayson."

"Hi, Grayson, I'm Forest. What can I do for you?" said Forest in his sweetest customer-service voice.

"Oh, dude, I think the question is, what can I do for you!" Grayson answered.

Forest offered Grayson his second-best fake laugh: "Heh heh." Then, "Tell me what you have in mind."

"Dude, you're not going to believe it. Grayson's Gym is opening a few blocks from you. We've got state-of-the art equipment, but, more than that, we have a 21st-century approach to fitness. All clients will receive wearable technology and personal, one-on-one coaching, and a required Fitness for Mental Health class. ChatGPT will now run all our classes so that we can tailor every workout to the exact needs of the client. We've got a juice bar with all-organic cleanses, twenty-four-seven meditation room, virtual fitness options every hour of day and night, onsite financial planners, group deep needling, liver detoxes, and special programs for toddlers, tweens, and Gen Alpha. Everyone will get the first year free. We're a franchise of Fierce Fitness, and I know you know about them." (Fierce Fitness was a global chain notorious for reducing gyms like Forest's to parking lots.)

"That all sounds wonderful. I know the community will be so pleased to have a resource like that in the area," Forest lied.

"Now, I want to be careful how I say this since I don't want to create any bad blood, but it's possible that Grayson's might cut into your client base. If you don't want to see your gym fade to nothing, I thought I could offer you a position with customer service. I'm sure the salary would be comparable to what you make at this little place."

"Wow, that's so kind of you to offer," said Forest, with "little place" stinging hard. "Customer service is my strong suit, and I can imagine how helpful it would be at a place like the one you describe. What's your timeline?"

"We open in about a month. We're planning a spectacular grand opening. The town will hold a parade, the mayor will speak, and, dude, get this: Jillian Michaels herself (THE Jillian Michaels) will do some live classes for us. We, of course, matched her salary. We're expecting about 30,000 visits in the first week or so."

"So amazing. I wish you lots of luck. It's exciting to see all this happening here."

"I agree. It's time for this town to have a really first-rate gym. No disrespect, dude, but how long has your little place been around? I took a look-see, and, I mean, the eighties are calling, and they want their equipment back. If I were you, I'd be thinking about how to move on."

"That's so helpful. I'm grateful to you for giving me a heads-up."

"Absolutely, positively, dude—the least I can do."

"Just a tiny question. Will your gym have a pool?"

Grayson flinched in a way imperceptible to most people but that Forest saw loud and clear. "Large jacuzzi, but no actual swimming pool. The cost of insuring a large pool is just too much, so we cut it. I think that with all the other features we have going, it will hardly be missed."

"That may be. I'll think about your offer, which I appreciate so much. If it's okay with you, I have to work on some scheduling issues right now."

"I understand," Grayson said. "Thanks so much for our chat. Loved seeing your little place."

Forest, remembering attacks of IBS that had been more fun than this meeting, knew the subtext, and knew that Grayson knew that he knew. Year after year, he had gone to national conferences of gym owners: "Fierce is killing us. We're not gonna last the year." Fierce's gyms had so many kettlebells and coaching whistles that customers could not wait to empty their wallets. It's not as if Forest's gym ever made much money (Grayson was right about the cost of insuring a pool, especially one with a deep end). And if what Grayson said was true, Forest's Fitness and Pool was facing an end as tragic as *Brokeback Mountain.*

But Forest had no time to brood, much as he wanted to. A noisy crowd had gathered outside his door. As he knew from emails, a lifeguard had called in sick; no backup because no lifeguards; no open pool; lots of angry clients. They formed two groups: rail-thin alpha swimmers (hairless twentysomethings wearing Speedos that left little to imagination) and the ferocious water fitness devotees. Next to these groups, the zombie horde in *28 Days Later* was *Romper Room*: "Why am I paying for a membership if this is going to happen?"

"Will you refund the class fee? I paid extra for this."

"You're here. Can't you just be a lifeguard" (Forest would have done so, but lifeguards needed to put their heads underwater, and a tube in his right ear kept him from submerging.) Not since the sinking of the *Lusitania* went down had there been an aquatic disaster on this scale.

Forest faced the crowd, gave a "safety first" speech, answered questions, thanked them for their concern, repeated the "safety first" speech, and the crowd, bored into submission, dispersed. Once again, he swore to himself he would advertise for a new lifeguard, though, when he found someone qualified, they were quickly snatched up by better-paying pools. At least the fitness center looked calm, with the regulars: Mauricio, bench pressing millions of pounds; Brianna, pounding on the treadmill as if she had no knees; Millie on the exercise bike, slow and steady, with her walker next to her; Ed grunting as if flames were coming out of his rear; DeWayne on the elliptical, chanting with his favorite rappers. And there was Zach, the trans guy from the other day. He smiled and gave Forest a thumbs-up. Forest would hold on to that—it meant that today would not be all bad, despite Grayson. His gym mattered, at least for some. And Forest heard music from the exercise studio, which meant that Jill had started her Turbo-Charged Zumba class, one of the best attended classes at the gym. Whatever Forest's opinions about Zumba (which he kept to himself), it brought people in. On land, all was calm; on water, a new lifeguard would start her shift in three hours, and the *Lusitania* would ride again.

And so the day went, one brushfire after the next, with financial doom looming over it all. Should Forest let the staff know about Grayson's? If he did, they'd probably leave… but the way Grayson talked, they'd leave anyway, sooner or later. He'd think about it later. Time now to greet the evening staff before he left for the day: Debra at the front desk,

Manuel in the fitness center, and Isaac as the sanitation engineer, a jewel. Isaac knew everybody's name and talked with everyone as they entered and left. He stayed late to make sure that the gym was spotless, which involved cleaning God knows what out of the lockers, checking all the weights were put away, cleaning bathrooms once again, making sure shower stalls were spotless and liquid soap refilled, checking that all fitness machines worked, locking doors and setting alarms, and locking the place securely. He had a habit of growling that took a while to get used to, but most at the gym had heard the occasional soft "grrrr" from him so often that they hardly noticed. Forest trusted no one more than Isaac and shuddered to think that Grayson's could entail firing Isaac if he did not leave on his own.

The whole day had gone by, and Forest still had not looked at Grant's message. Going back to his apartment was another chance to delay. Although on the map his apartment was a short hop from the gym, Pine Rapids' investment in bike lanes had turned an easy drive into a World War I reenactment. Not because of bikes, mind you (nobody used the bike lanes because Pine Rapids was a frozen hellscape in February), but because of other cars struggling with a two-lane road remodeled into a one-lane road, on which cars had to park, plus a deserted bike lane. Forest preferred unplowed back streets as an alternative because they had less traffic, though more treacherous snow. In his sad used Pluto, a car so unloved that the manufacturer had halted production a year ago, he lumbered over glaciers and crept along snowy mounds until he reached home.

As usual the elevator took forever, so he climbed the stairs and arrived, huffing, at his apartment. Mothra immediately started an arioso about Forest's shocking neglect in not feeding her immediately. She calmed down once she received her usual Fancy Feast (grilled, not pate), so Forest could finally collapse into his falling-apart chair and thank God for inventing DoorDash. Vietnamese it was.

Having gotten his order off (spring rolls and mock duck with potatoes), he avoided dealing with Grant by doing what any self-respecting gay man would do: waste time with hookup apps. He was most active on Inchz because it had the fewest bots and gorgeous models usually located in the greater Accra region of Ghana. The Inchz icon appeared on the screen, a ruler with a beam of light that progressed along the animated ruler inch by inch. Suddenly, instead of the usual array of suspects, most of whom Forest knew by heart, a prerecorded video popped up. Was this some promotional stunt by Inchz? But there, unbelievably, was Grant's face. Forest took a second to register what was happening. How had Grant taken over Inchz?

"Hey, Forest, didn't want you to think that you hadn't made an impression. Here are some pics and my number. Call me." And then the video disappeared, and a file emerged with pictures and Grant's name. Forest had a choice to make. He could give Mothra the attention she was demanding, plan his exercise classes for the next day, or inspect Grant's pictures. Very closely. He made the right choice. Upon inspection, Grant was toned without being muscle bound, hairy without being a yeti, older without being shriveled. Grant included both older and younger photos, and somehow he looked better as he aged. He had lost a tragic mustache, and his face had become leaner and more focused. Forest felt his palms getting sweaty as he looked.

To Forest's relief, no hint of green anywhere, just a healthy tan. He did notice faint indentations near Grant's shoulder blades, whose origin was not clear. Forest chose to ignore them. Maybe they were just scars. They didn't look like scars, but it didn't seem as if they could be anything else.

Even better, Grant wanted to meet him again. He told him to call. Forest grabbed his phone. And then put it down. And then stared at it. And then grabbed it and put it down again. *Don't screw it up, don't screw it up*, echoed in his head. Forest sighed. He would screw it up. It probably would not last more than one or two dates, but it would not hurt, at least not too much, and he might have some fun along the way. And he was curious.

And so, plunged into a reverie of overthinking, he stared at his phone. Suddenly, Anita Ward started singing "Ring My Bell," and Forest jumped. His phone was ringing. It never rang, so he was caught off guard. In his surprise, all knowledge of how to use a smartphone evaporated. But, somehow, he heard Grant's voice.

Grant: "Good evening, Forest? Art thou there?"

Forest: (fumbling while muttering obscenities).

Grant: "I hear something, but I'm not sure thou'rt coming through."

Forest: (pulls up by mistake a random embarrassing TikTok; more obscenities)

Grant: "Forest?"

Forest: (trying to swipe right but sweating so much that the screen would not move)

Grant: "Well, I guess thou'rt not there. I'll retry later."

Forest: Internal Fay Wray scream: "F*****."

Grant: "Bye for now."

Forest: "NOOOOOO. Hold on just a second"—and, miraculously, he found the right screen and pressed the Accept button. "Grant, Grant, Grant, are you there?" (pant, gasp, pant, gasp).

Grant: "Forest!"

Forest: "So sorry! I was just about to burn dinner and needed a second." Was it possible to be a worse liar?

Grant: "I was just wondering if thou mightst have dinner with me. There's a restaurant Italian nearby, and I thought it would be a delight to pass time."

Forest: (desperate. but not wanting to appear so): "That sounds fun, but my week is a little busy. When did you have in mind?"

Grant: "Perhaps Wednesday? I could pick thee up if thou wishest to give me thy address."

Forest: "Let me check." Forest put the phone down and, paying homage to the god of hypocrisy, looked at his empty calendar. He walked back. And took a second before answering. "We're in luck! I'm free then. Is six thirty good for you? I know it's on the early side, but I have to get up early for the gym."

Grant: "See you then."

And that was that. Only after it was over did Forest realize that he had not given Grant an address. He had killed the date before it had even begun—and with the hottest guy he had ever seen. But he couldn't help overthinking anyway. What would he wear? Not too dressy (shades of Ray), but not a slob. Grant might want sex (seemed fair), but just how far would they go? Would the earlyish dinner hour mean that they'd be spared live music, which was only slightly less effective than strychnine for killing a vibe? And, toughest question, what would he eat? Pizza was too obvious, but something he'd actually like, such as pesto or gnocchi, had garlic H-bomb potential. And what about the mess? A calzone leaked faster than nuclear waste; twirling spaghetti on a fork created a scary blob of carb; chewing meatballs looked too suggestive.

Forest snapped himself out of his reverie. Grant did not even have his address. This date was not likely to happen. But a little hopeful voice inside said, *Grant somehow took over all of Inchz just to send you a video message. He should have no trouble finding your address. There aren't that many Forests in Pine Rapids. He'll find you.* Even as Forest berated himself for being absurd, he clung to hope.

CHAPTER 6

"IT'S NOT as if I'm leaving. I'll just be working at two gyms," Jill said.

"But Grayson's isn't just any other gym. It's out to kill me. You'll be making three times what I can pay you," said Forest, sensing that Jill's departure was the beginning of the end.

"I have a dedicated group here, and I'm not abandoning them. I'll still teach my class. I'll just be teaching other classes at Grayson's. It's not as if fitness instructors have noncompete clauses."

"But you'll be a double agent!" cried Forest. "You'll be able to share with them all the things that make my gym special. And I expect that you'll tell me what specials they're offering to lure our members."

"Forest!" she snapped. "We're talking about a Zumba class, not James Bond. It's just not that big a deal. And it's not really your decision."

It was not his decision, but it was his business, since Forest was soon going to watch his beloved gym be Death Starred by Grayson's. He was so upset about his looming professional collapse that he had less time than usual to overthink his date with Grant. But when Wednesday finally arrived, all his past bad dates haunted him. He remembered Tp4Btm, who had broken his heart. They had developed a good rapport on Inchz (translation: Tp4Btm produced strings of almost grammatical sentences), had exchanged pics, and had found a date/time that worked. Forest had scrubbed himself, scrubbed Mothra, scrubbed the apartment. And then, silence. Forest was left to mourn the death of his hopes and his erection.

Later that evening, Tp4Btm messaged that something had come up at the last minute. Forest fumed. What could possibly be more important than a sex date with him? He knew he needed to care less. At least Tp4Btm should have messaged him sooner. But that was not how the game was played.

By now, Forest knew that, with regard to gay dating apps, he should have the skin of a Gila monster or an aging California beach bunny. But here he was again, hoping and crushing hope, daydreaming and snapping back to reality, letting his imagination soar and scolding himself for being a fool. He supposed no date would ever ghost Grayson. Grayson, unlike Forest, was a guy for whom people showed up.

For a bottom, a gay date had its own ten commandments:

1. Thou shalt not wear anything hard to take off.

2. Thou shalt douche more than thou thinkest thou hast to.

3. Honor thy tight pants and keep them ready.

4. Thou shalt not use scent.

5. Thou shalt find a way to brush teeth and use mouthwash after food.

6. Thou shalt not shave sloppily.

7. Thou shalt honor thy lower regions (=sphincter) and keep them clean.

8. Thou shalt not order Mexican fool.

9. Thy hair shalt not feel like the Exxon Valdez.

10. Honor thy top by letting him think he's doing all the work.

But the commandments left open a key question for a bottom: underwear or not? Wearing no underwear at all sent a message. In theory, he knew that some tops would prefer that bottoms have underwear so they could take it off. But underwear removal in theory is not underwear removal in practice. What should be a smooth, sexy maneuver too often turned into the epitome of awkwardness. Years of gay experience had taught Forest that wisdom lay in going commando.

Forest's choice, however, was not risk-free since everyone has seen *There's Something About Mary*. As a bottom, it was the law that he had to wear tight pants (cf. the Third Commandment). Any top wanted a preview of coming attractions, so it seemed only fair. But tight pants made it hard to position a zipper to avoid repeating Ben Stiller. Maybe just wear sweatpants? No, bad call. Grant invited him to dinner, and it was part of an unwritten contract that Forest had to look presentable. And so, like so many bottoms before him, he agonized by weighing zipper catastrophe against bubble-butt appeal.

Nobody looks good in turtlenecks, but they somehow worked for Forest. He had a long neck, and turtlenecks made it look sleek instead of giraffey. Since turtlenecks violated the "must come off easily" of the First Commandment, Forest had mastered getting them off fast (deep chin tuck, collar up and over the nose, then a firm grip on the collar to let the whole thing slide up and over. He even adapted this move for his fitness classes). Final touch: a tiny bit of concealer. Gay men should never be quite honest about their faces. It looks so calculating. He surveyed the *tout ensemble* in the mirror. Chris Hemsworth had nothing to worry about, but a charitable judge might give him an okay.

Since he hadn't left any contact information for Grant, there was no way for him to tell Forest just when he might arrive. And Forest had no clue about contacting Grant, who had never volunteered so much as an Instagram link. Just to be on the safe side, Forest was ready at five thirty, much, much sooner than he had to be. How would it end? Would they really have sex, and, if so, what would it mean? Or just a chaste peck on the cheek? What if they hated each other? Who would pay for the food? What would they talk about? What if he smelled bad?

Forest glued himself to his apartment window waiting for a car to appear—not that he knew what Grant's car would look like, but he could guess. 6:00, 6:05, 6:10—nothing. Forest was entering the risky zone, that band of time when hope is not quite gone but consolation speeches begin to bubble up. When a car pulled up in front of the building, he flew downstairs, only to see Marley and Barbara, the twin six-year-olds from the third floor, coming back all beribboned and be-tutued from ballet class. Embarrassed, Forest pretended to check his mail. To his surprise, he saw a tiny note in his box on paper so thin that it was almost tissue: "See you at 6:15—Grant."

At that moment, Forest heard a bell ring from outside. He turned and froze, staring at the most beautiful car he had ever seen——so beautiful that it did not even honk. This car made Forest's miserable Pluto look worse than the Joads' truck. But this car had it all. It was sleek, stylish, a little retro chic. Lost in wonder, Forest jumped a bit when a window rolled down and he heard Grant's voice say, "Hop in! Great to see thee!"

What Forest thought: *Don't look desperate, don't look desperate. My walk is too swishy. No, it's too butch. I can't be sending the right signals. I think I'm desperately trying to look not desperate. I'm about to trip and fall on my face. My armpits are pouring like Niagara. Am I really the kind of guy who has sex in exchange just for an Italian dinner?* (An easy "yes," since plenty of men offered a lot less.) *I'm going to make a complete idiot of myself, and my shoes are about to fall off—these were so the wrong socks.*

What Forest said, smiling: "Great to see you! I'm looking forward to this."

And they were off.

To Forest's amazement, the date went well—actually, better than well. They had a small table tucked away in a corner, where they could talk without feeling that straight people were judging them ("Oh, that's the aging queens' table"). Grant ordered Roman chicken; Forest (after much thought) settled on veal scallopini (no messy spaghetti! no garlic overload!). Grant was easy to talk to. He asked about Forest's apartment, how long he had lived in Pine Rapids, his strategies for negotiating the winter, his favorite places in the city… nothing original or even brilliant, but also nothing embarrassing or scary. Forest felt himself, to his surprise, relax. He realized how tense he had felt with Ray, who so loved a little dig, a casual putdown, a last word.

"I'm worried about my gym. A snazzy new one is opening up close by, and I think it's going to run me into the ground," Forest confessed.

"Oh no! What can I do to help?"

"The one thing I've got that the new gym won't have is a big pool. It's a huge pain in the rear to keep up, but the people who like it are my best customers. If I could get a large influx of new clients who wanted to use the pool, I'd be getting a different market sector. That would be my best shot at long-term survival."

"Done."

"Done?" laughed Forest. "You mean you can make new clients appear out of thin air?"

"Who said anything about thin air? But I have ideas about how to get thee new clients."

Was this guy for real? Ray had yawned at anything Forest said about his gym. Forest found himself wanting to tell Grant everything on his mind about the gym, from lifeguards to instructors to looming collapse. But for all his faults, he knew enough not to spend the whole time talking about his own problems.

"Okay, if you say so. It seems only fair for me to ask if there's anything I can do for you?"

Grant's eyebrows arched at this, and Forest realized exactly how his question might sound. He watched the shadow of a smile playing on Grant's lips, but, instead of the lewd suggestion that most guys would have made, he took his time before saying, "Yes, actually there is."

"Name it," said Forest.

"There's a dangerous group that has arrived in Pine Rapids. I'm not sure what they're calling themselves or where they are located. But they are a serious threat, especially to local children. For reasons I don't want to go into, the police will not be effective against them."

"Okay," said Forest, wondering where this was going.

"All I ask is that thou keepest thy ears open. As the owner of a gym, thou meetest all kinds of people in the course of the day. Let me know if anyone says anything about seeing a strange group of individuals or, even more seriously, if any threats are made against any children."

Forest's gut told him to say no, since he retreated from anything that sounded like conflict. But Grant had offered to help him, and he felt he should reciprocate. And, after all, it wasn't much of an ask. It's not as if he had to do anything, just notice what he noticed. He sensed that Grant, mysterious as he was, was worried and wanted to do the right thing. Anyway, given the likely fate of his gym, he needed all the friends he could make. If Grant was able to get him new clients, then anything he asked in return would be worth it. Forest, without knowing he had done it, had just taken a big step.

Time flew, and before Forest knew what was happening, dinner was over, Grant drove him home, gave him the chastest of pecks on his cheek, and deposited him at his apartment. Forest hadn't made a fool of himself, dropped his food, belched or farted at inopportune moments. He had provided coherent, even logical responses to Grant's questions. No awkward pauses. No catastrophic encounters with waitstaff. No awkward questions about what comes next.

And yet, though Forest could not admit it to himself, part of him was a tiny bit disappointed. He had wanted Grant to be more aggressive, even though he was happy that he hadn't been. He had been curious (very) about what sex with Grant might be like, even as he was relieved it hadn't happened. The chaste peck had been so, so chaste. He would not have hated the teensiest bit more (maybe a bit of tongue?). Couldn't he have had just a minute or two, perhaps, to explore Grant's body, even if things went no further than petting? And, perhaps most of all, no next-date plans, even though Grant had asked him to keep his eyes open and promised to help the gym. It had been a lovely evening, and that, sigh, was that.

CHAPTER 7

Forest was not going to turn into one more boy waiting for the phone to ring. He and Grant had had fun on Wednesday, and that, evidently, was that. Nothing kinky, nothing untoward… sigh. Forest felt just as he had the first time with Grant. Grant was present when he was present, and it was over when it was over.

Forest threw himself into work, was extra-energetic in his classes, was super-nice to all the members, supported the staff, and oversaw the flood of work-related administrivia as if it were interesting. And when he got home, he collapsed into a heap of self-pity. If Grant had actually stood him up or broken a promise, it would be one thing. Then he could be angry. But Grant had behaved perfectly, and Forest could not forgive him.

As he told Mothra, "What gets to me is the uncertainty."

Mothra returned a cold stare of indifference, as if to say, "I worry about the uncertainty of when you will feed me, but I manage."

Forest continued, "If I had wanted uncertainty, I'd have been a stockbroker or at least a southern Californian. I need at least some predictability."

"Just feed me several times a day. What more predictability does anyone need?"

Was the right next move to talk to Grant about this (if he ever gave Forest a way to contact him) or just to dump him and move on? There wasn't much to dump since it's not as if Grant had asked him to be his boyfriend. In terms of sex, they had been as pure as Puritans. Wasn't Forest just getting ahead of himself in thinking through all this? And did he really want an "honesty" conversation in which he had to tell a partner what the partner should have known anyway?

Mothra condescended to note, "Grant can't read your mind; I, in contrast, could, but why would I put myself through that?"

"I'm aware," said Forest, still thinking that it hardly required Dear Abby-level acuity to know that leaving someone clueless about when you would next see them was irritating. In fact, the more Forest thought about it, the angrier he became.

His phone buzzed; he had a message.

"Hey, it's Grant. Maybe Greek food Saturday night? See thee at 7 pm."

In a rush of joyful panic, Forest texted back immediately: "Sire!"

He froze.

What had he just done? Whoever had put the "u" and the "i" so close together on the keyboard better be doing extra time in Purgatory.

The full realization of just how his typo looked hit him like a ton of rainbow-color bricks. Embarrassment grabbed the pit of his stomach as he underwent multiple agonizing shame-deaths in succession. He who sneered at others for typos and bad syntax had just made a complete fool out of himself (again). And it was an accident: he had meant to type something else. What would Grant think? That he was just giving back nonsense? That Forest was making fun of Grant for his bossiness? That he was incapable of responding in a way that made any sense at all?

With a sheepish sigh, Forest texted, "Oops! I meant 'sure.'"

After a pause, when Forest tried to look anywhere except at his screen but found that his eyes nevertheless locked there, he saw Grant's response: "I figured."

Forest breathed a sigh of relief. And then, quickly: "Though I didn't mind."

OMG, how should he respond to that? Mental distress signals competed with very enjoyable reverie about Grant's sire potential, with his thighs and slightly weird green torso....

But he had to answer. "Thanks?" "Ok?" "LOL?" (nobody used "LOL" anymore). Smiley face? Smiley face with tears? Some random emoji, maybe a donut? After scrolling through hundreds of options in less than eight seconds, he settled on, "I'd love to hear more," followed by a winky smiley face. Using emojis took more concentration than inventing the iPhone.

As opposed to his first date with Grant, when Forest was not even sure that he would show up, he at least knew that Grant could find him and had a specific time to show up. All the fretting that Forest had at first put into wondering if Grant would show he now put into overthinking every nanosecond of the upcoming date. Yes, the first date with Grant had been fun. But what if it was just a fluke? He was haunted by a fitness industry maxim: you're only as good as your last class. What if the chemistry between him and Grant was just a one-time, never to be repeated thing, like a Ryan Gosling full frontal? And if Italian food had been a challenge, Greek food was a whole new kettle of calamari.

Forest spent most of Saturday lost in planning, worry, and speculation: same clothes/different clothes? Same hair/different hair? Same shoes/different shoes (an easy one—he only had one pair). What would they talk about? Hadn't they run out of everything easy to talk about already? And who'd pay for dinner? Grant had paid at the first date and didn't even ask for sex in return, which was one for the history books. But Forest couldn't expect him to pay again. He was not a boytoy, at least not yet—no point in ruling anything out in advance. Though Forest's gym was not exactly a cash cow, especially now that it was on the verge of collapse, he could afford dinner out, even with two people.

Grant would cancel at the last minute. Forest would get into a fight with the waiter (he was still smarting from his Cabin Coffee humiliation). Grant would lean in for a kiss, and Forest would burp. And then, the Big Question: sex afterward or not? A chaste first date was nice, if a bit unusual; a sexless second date was unheard of. And if Greek food was a minefield, Greek love was a whole galaxy of potential catastrophe. What queer theorists talked about the real issues: getting hair in your teeth, not getting the penetration angle quite right, inhibiting a choke response during oral sex (to say nothing of teeth), or discovering too late that fingernails were sharper than anticipated? It took all the magic of porn to make it look like this was easy.

And, again, Forest's fret turned out to be for nothing. Once the date started, everything fell into place. Grant arrived, the restaurant was lovely, the food was perfect, and the conversation flowed as if they had known each other much longer than they had. Once again, Forest was amazed that a date could actually be fun. But even still, he could not stop the Demon of Overthinking Everything from lurking in the back of his mind. This time, the issue was what would happen after dinner, or, as Forest liked to think of it, as dessert: just how would sex be after dinner? Whose place would they go to? What did Grant's place look like, and was everything green there too? If they went to Forest's apartment, would they fit on Forest's twin bed? Grant was a big guy and he might just inadvertently roll off—or, more likely, take up so much space that Forest would end up under the bed.

This potentially endless train of speculation halted when Grant asked, seemingly out of the blue, "Wouldst thou wish to visit Sweatshop after dinner?" Forest practically spit out his spanakopita. Sweatshop! Well, that answered the sex question but opened up whole new paths for fretting. Sweatshop was town's most notorious (and only) gay bath. It had closed at the height of the pandemic, and Forest had wondered, as had most of gay Pine Rapids, if it might close for good. Many months must have gone by when it was not making money. But it turns out that it was eligible for small-business support, and, since maintenance was not too expensive, it weathered the pandemic storm better than anyone expected. When it reopened, Pine Rapids' gay community reembraced it with joyful abandon. It became even more popular than it had been pre-pandemic, as if public sex was a badge of being officially over the pandemic.

Forest had been to Sweatshop a few times before the pandemic but never really got into it for the same reason that he avoided bars. He couldn't hear anything over the blasting music. He was old-fashioned enough to care about what other people were saying, and the noise demolished that option. He admitted that there were fun things about Sweatshop, including scoping out a lot of guys in a short time—definitely worth the price of admission. But the pandemic had kept him away, and Ray had never been interested. Ray was far above Sweatshop and spoke condescendingly of how abject it was next to the glories of real bathhouses like Chicago's Steamworks or Montreal's G. I. Joe.

And now Grant wanted to go, and Forest was 100 percent unprepared. Not unwilling, exactly, just unprepared. Sweatshop's number one rule was a strict one: no clothes. Like a queer *Hitchhiker's Guide to the Galaxy*, you were allowed a towel, but that was it. Forest always kept his shoes on as well because the floors of a bathhouse did not hold up well on close inspection. With his skin chalky white, his underarms pouring sweat, and his heart pounding out of his chest, he said to Grant, "What a great idea! I'd love to." Grant reached over to take his hand and did not seem to notice either that Forest's hand was moister than Desdemona's or that his sleeve had had a dodgy encounter with the tzatziki.

CHAPTER 8

DAY FOLLOWED day with no contact from the Quyre, until one evening, when Ray was worn out from a full day of online shopping, their faces appeared again on his computer. Eelie went straight to the point:

"We thought you'd like to see some live feed of the last guy who failed us." Ray's computer went blank and was soon replaced by a streaming video of a tiny cabin in an endless waste of snow. Chained to a wood-burning stove that maintained only the lowest of embers, a man shivered and cried. His face was raw, his frost-bitten hands were turning black, and he looked as if he had not eaten in weeks. Uncomfortable as the scene looked, Ray soon realized that the cold was not the worst. Muzak played in the background, with frequent interruptions of "We're sorry for the delay. A member of our staff will be with you shortly." It never stopped.

Ray, unexpectedly gripped by what he saw in front of him, muttered, "Food?"

The Quyre responded indifferently, "Gerber baby food's sweet potato turkey dinner with whole grains and gravy, washed down with Manischewitz." Ray crumpled, overwhelmed with horror.

The next morning, haunted by dreams of cold weather, baby food, and Muzak, he took his first step. After a brief Google search, he telephoned on his mobile:

"Good morning. McNaughten-Steg school. How may I help you?"

"I'm picking up a friend's child from McNaughten-Steg this afternoon and wanted to understand how dismissal from school worked for the preschoolers."

McNaughton-Steg was the prestige school in Pine Rapids. Everyone who was anyone made sure that their kid was in it. Its website showed preschoolers in a hive of activity. Ray vaguely remembered having played with blocks in nursery school but had learned from the website that these kids spent their days analyzing genomic data on chicken pox and croup, using 3-D printers to develop self-driving tricycles, and learning Sibelius to compose their own music, which had produced several viral hits on Tik Tok.

"Preschoolers who stay for the day are dismissed at three thirty. But if you are not the regular parent or care provider, you will come to the office at noon for an evaluation of your suitability to take the child. We'll examine legal records, do a complete physical, lie detector test, drug analysis, psychiatric evaluation, and driver's test. In addition we'll need your birth certificate, marriage license if applicable, vaccination records, insurance documents...." Ray realized that this was going to be harder than he thought but decided just to show up at three thirty to see what might happen.

When he arrived a few hours later, even a block from the school, he saw rows of Teslas, Maseratis, and Rolls-Royces, all the size of small luxury cruise ships. The value of the parental rolling stock edged out the GDP of Rhode Island. Ray watched carefully from the street as the kids were dismissed. Police cars arrived soon to block off roads leading to and from the school. A small army of suits gathered at the entrance; police cars lined the parking lot. Ray heard the flutter of helicopters overhead. After prolonged negotiations, a small mob of armed servicemen moved in unison to different parental cars. At each car, another negotiation proceeded, after which the armed corps parted briefly to allow a toddler into a car—not that Ray ever saw a child. As soon as the child had been deposited, the car zoomed off at Fast and Furious speeds.

Snatching one of these kids would be as easy as grabbing a crucifix off the Pope. McNaughton-Steg guarded its preschoolers with the most up-to-date resources of the military-industrial complex. Ray's visit was enlightening, but not helpful. As the Quyre said, he had only two weeks, and obtaining a Product seemed as unlikely as ever. A lifetime of cold Muzak stretched before him.

Ray still had no Product and his likelihood of living to an age when ED might be a worry was shrinking with every passing hour. All local preschools had dismissal procedures that made D-Day look like amateur hour. The Quyre continued to send him bullying encouragement. Although he had long since deposited most of their money, he had gotten used to other items in his apartment berating him for his delay: his coffee mug, his razor, his hand sanitizer. If Ray had known anything about *Hamlet*, he would have said that killing Claudius would have been a snap, but kidnapping a preschooler—now that was hard.

Feeling sorry for himself, Ray wandered to Cabin Coffee. He knew that this late in the morning, Forest was not likely to be there, so he could be alone. Two women were talking as if the entire coffee shop had to be part of the conversation:

"Rhonda actually pulled Luna out of preschool!"

"I know! But it had never occurred to her that Luna wouldn't be learning to code. All the other preschools offer it."

"Exactly. It's just expected these days. I've seen it on every parenting forum."

"When Rhonda confronted Mrs. Vitelli, can you believe what she said?"

"OMG. What?"

"AI would be taking over all the coding jobs in the future. What children needed to learn now was to interact with other people."

"Huh?"

"I know, I know. If all the nursery school teachers felt like that, who is going to code the AI?"

"To be fair, kids love the school. They have a great time, and Mrs. Vitelli does try to get them to be nice. But kids are always going to be bullies, and discipline is our job as mothers. We send them to preschool for academics (sympathetic nods from other mother), and they just aren't there."

"Well I think Rhonda was right. No more Montessori for Luna. Do you know where she's going to go?"

As Ray listened, it sounded as if the name of the no-coding school was "Collie Montessori." Was Luna a dog? That may be why Mrs. Vitelli was not keen on coding. He imagined wealthy Lassies trotting off to elite classrooms. "Montessori" smelled of privilege. Those were lucky dogs. Since he had become an expert on preschool dismissal, Collie Montessori piqued his curiosity mostly because he had never heard of it before.

If Collie Montessori prioritized letting its students, who might not even be kids, play, it might have a less rigorous dismissal procedure. Maybe its battalion of special agents would be smaller? If it indeed had kids and not dogs, maybe swiping one would not make too much of a ripple? Unfortunately, "Collie Montessori" produced nothing on Google. But when asked about Montessori schools in Pine Rapids, it showed "Kali Montessori," and Ray realized his mistake. It was not a school for Lassie but one named after the Hindu goddess of war. Ray thought it was a strange name but perused the Google reviews to learn more about it: "The kids just play together." "Shockingly unrigorous. No classes in coding, biogenetics, or advanced Cornish. How can children learn?" "The 4-year-olds could read not much more than the alphabet and a few short words." An occasional positive review ("My daughter had a wonderful time at Kali. She learned to treat children her own age with care and respect") was lost in a flood of condemnation. Ray, irritated that nobody mentioned how Kali dismissed children—why did people never focus on what mattered?—still felt curious. The dogs of war at Kali might be pussycats.

When Ray drove to the school, it turned out to be a nondescript building on a nondescript street. The back was a vacant lot. No expensive playground equipment, no pool, no hockey rink. If, as Ray suspected, this place added thousands to tuition by using the word "Montessori," the money did not go into appearance. It had zero curb appeal. This made Ray happy.

Ray came back at dismissal time, between three and four. Instead of the highly coordinated SWAT teams at the other schools, this school just let successive mobs of kids out. There was some attention to making sure that the kids did not all leave at once, but once they were out of the school, they were on their own. Some had parents to pick them up, but others seemed to be walking home on their own. Quite a few went to the lot in the back to play, despite the lack of fancy equipment.

Thinking about the threats of the Quyre, Ray imagined making an inconspicuous grab. It would be better not to do it right in front of the school, where other parents were. Waiting until a kid was on a side street seemed smarter. But what if he couldn't grab the kid? Or if he did, what would he do with it? Putting it in the trunk was a terrible idea. He had seen too many movies in which people escaped from trunks by kicking down the back seat. Maybe if he just dumped the kid in the back seat? But wouldn't it crawl around? What if it tried to get out again? In the movies, kidnappers had chloroform—but where in the world would he get that? And wouldn't it be a huge mess? Given all the complexities and difficulties, Ray did what he usually did: ignored them.

Two days later, Ray returned. It was now or never. He lurked on a side street, though not one he had been on before. Even when children walked by his car, just grabbing a kid and taking off bothered him. It seemed messy, to say nothing of illegal. Yes, the Quyre were forcing him to do this, and, yes, he wanted the reward, but he really was not having fun. He got out of the car and carefully placed his large pistachio latte with coconut milk, warm, but not hot, 5 ¼ pumps of pistachio sauce, substitute caramel drizzle, and light pistachio cream cold foam on top of the car while he adjusted his coat. As he turned to retrieve his coffee, his foot slipped on the curb, and, as he flung his arms out to steady himself, he managed to knock the entire latte onto himself.

"Dammit," he said as he sprang backward away from the car and stumbled away a little bit too hard, which led to him landing with a resounding thump where the sun doesn't shine (except during his luxury vacations to nude beaches in the Mediterranean). Well, at least this was a quiet street, so nobody saw him. He took off his coat and began flapping it to get as much coffee off as possible. It was a big-ticket coat, and having it wrecked would hurt. He looked ridiculous, but he didn't care.

But was he so alone? As he was flapping his coat, he heard a strange, high-pitched sound. He looked around and saw a small child not far away (where had it come from?), laughing fit to burst. "Silly! Silly!" said the child, who seemed to be male, repeatedly. Ray realized that the entire coffee disaster, which to him was a tragedy of epic proportions, was more entertaining than the Power Rangers for this toddler. "Silly!" The toddler laughed and then started to imitate Ray. He pulled off his jacket and started shaking it in every direction imaginable, along with more giggles. To Ray's horror, the child was coming closer to him and his car.

But what happened next was completely unexpected. "Car!" yelled the toddler. Using both his tiny fists, he yanked open the back door of Ray's car and dove in, still waving his jacket everywhere. Ray looked at the muddy shoes and overall filthiness of the toddler's clothes, fists, and face, and moved immediately to haul him out. But as soon as he touched the toddler, it screamed loud enough to wake up Republicans during a Democratic State of the Union address. Ray drew back. What could he do?

Just then, the Quyre appeared from nowhere. "The Product! The Product!" they shrieked. For all his thoughts of revenge upon children, when it came to the moment, he did not want them to get the kid. But then it occurred to him that they would at least get the kid out of his nice car, and he wanted that very much.

"Take him. Just get him out of my car."

"Oh no," mumbled Eelie, "that's not how this works."

"Huh?"

Kid quieted down and seemed to settle into Ray's car.

"The Rite is in two weeks. We cannot touch the Product until the Rite."

"Well, that's your problem. I promised you the Product. Here it is. I did not promise to keep it for you until whenever."

"We built in buffer time in case you failed to get the Product and had to be eliminated."

"Again, your problem. I got the Product; it's here. Take it and leave."

Eelie's eyes flared. He certainly did not appreciate being told to get lost from a mere human like Ray. He was preparing a crushing reply when Fennel intervened: "Ray, it's only two weeks. It will fly by. I'm going to give you more of an advance now, and we will double our initial offer." Ray heard nothing except "advance" and "double… offer."

He took a deep breath. "Every policeman in town will be after this kid. There will be Amber Alerts, milk cartons, America's Most Wanted, and that's just for a start."

Fennel said, "Let that be our problem. Keep the Product safe for two weeks, and we'll handle the rest."

And thus Ray found himself driving back to his apartment with a noisy, semi-kidnapped toddler.

CHAPTER 9

FOREST'S HEART thumped all the way to Grant's car. Visions of catastrophe danced in his head. Grant would find Adonis or Ganymede (or both) at Sweatshop and leave with them; Forest would skulk home alone in a Lyft. Illogically, Forest also worried that it was too early to hit Sweatshop because it didn't fill until after eleven, so it would be a ghost town (with a disco soundtrack) at this time of night. But at least it was the weekend, and his gym was closed on Sundays, so he could hang with Grant for as long as he wanted. But what did Grant want? And just how was it going to happen? Sweatshop was a gay gothic castle, with dark galleries and unexpected doors and rooms appearing where there should not be rooms (except that these cost extra and had to be rented by the hour).

The ugly anteroom looked the same as it used to: fluorescent lighting, stark white walls with special events listed (*RuPaul's Drag Race* dominated every aspect of gay gatherings in Pine Rapids), bored-looking twink behind the desk, now with a big plexiglass screen because of COVID, the glamorless heap of towel/lock/key pushed through the window, and the same big door, painted leather black, with its stern "18 and Over Only" that gave entry to Sweatshop itself.

But once inside, Forest was surprised to find that Sweatshop had changed quite a bit. It had always been a maze, but it had exploded into labyrinths of options: the nonbinary wing; the genderqueer space; the room for the straight curious; the special section for vanilla leather (just what was that?), along with the more traditional BDSM rooms; anonymous sex for the trauma sensitive; asexual spaces for those who just wanted to talk. And everywhere, little posters proclaiming, "Consent first!" Forest had thought that showing up at Sweatshop implied consent (why else was anyone there?), but he supposed that this made sense to somebody. And as he thought about it, he remembered a night years ago at Sweatshop that, if not nonconsensual, wasn't exactly consensual either. It fell into that murk of regrettable, but not quite criminal encounters—just seriously icky. Would consent reminders have given him just a little more nerve on that night, just a tiny bit more guts to give Mr. Wrong the well-timed push he deserved? Too late now, but presumably enough similar encounters had happened at Sweatshop for "Consent first" to matter.

Grant led the way to the locker room, which, unlike most of Sweatshop, was actually well-lit so that you could see what you were doing as you undressed and locked up everything that you wanted to take home with you, except a man (wallet, phone, keys, etc.). It smelled just like the locker room at Forest's gym. The custodial people must use the same cleaners (which led Forest irrelevantly to imagine a huge vat of bathroom cleaner underlying the entire continental US, which custodians everywhere could tap into at any time just by turning a faucet). Pine Rapids wasn't exactly the crime capital of the world, and Sweatshop was probably pretty safe, but being gay never stopped a Miss Stickyfingers. Since Forest knew the glaring overhead light in the locker room was as good as it was going to get, he looked carefully at Grant. He had never seen him nude in real life and wondered just exactly what he would see, since Grant's pictures had been somewhat different from Grant over Zoom. His heart started to pound once again as Grant casually slipped off his clothes, and his knees went just a little bit weak. Forest was winning the Gay Cliche of the Night award. But Grant's body was so…. He grabbed his towel to hide obvious signs of his admiration. Grant didn't say anything, but Forest thought he saw a shadow of a smile flit across his face (the beard hid a lot).

But there it was again. Much as Forest would have preferred not to notice, he could not stop wondering. Grant's body still gave the spectral impression of greenness even though nothing about it was really green. Over Zoom, the color was some kind of weird tattoo or costume. Here, in the unforgiving fluorescence of Sweatshop, Grant's body was as breathtaking and as weird as ever. Forest stared as he tried to figure out just how the play of light and shadow on Grant's joints, muscles, tendons, and black-gray body hair created the impression of green even if, as soon as Forest focused on a single spot, there was no green at all. Green hovered in the periphery, always somewhere else on Grant's body. As soon as Forest tried to catch it, it disappeared.

Grant, carrying his towel ever so smoothly in his right hand, walked over to Forest, put out his arm, and said, "Shall we?" Forest was so dumfounded by having to take the arm of another man—who did that anymore?—that he could think of nothing to say and just walked with Grant into the bowels of Sweatshop. That was the end of his brief dermatological exam because suddenly, the presence or absence of his greenness hardly mattered. The lighting was haunted-house dark—just a few red bulbs flickered here and there to prevent you and the wall from having an unsatisfying hookup. The usual music was blaring (THUMP THUMP THUMP THUMP), and they passed into a dreamy nightmare world of dark hallways and almost-but-not-quite visible bodies. Now and then, they passed a little alcove, with benches against the walls and porn playing on TV. Forest did not understand why anyone would come to Sweatshop to watch porn, but it was probably best not to be too judgy in this place. Walking around stark naked in near total darkness leveled everybody and everything.

But there was more to these spaces than just watching. Forest had forgotten that these were also waiting areas. On the walls behind the benches were boards with red LED numbers that announced when a private room was available (after a maintenance person had cleaned—very thoroughly—whatever had happened among the previous users). It felt exactly like waiting for Patty and Selma at the Motor Vehicles Administration, except that the red numbers were smaller and darker—and you could watch porn. It could be a long wait, especially for some of the more desirable, more expensive rooms, so might as well have something to pass the time....

Forest was curious less about the private rooms, which he had seen before, than about the new spaces at Sweatshop. Just what exactly went on in them? Who got to decide the mechanics of the encounter in a nonbinary room? How much was planned in advance, and how much just happened spontaneously? Sweatshop being Sweatshop, Forest suspected that a lot must happen pretty spontaneously, but he really didn't know. And what rooms had been shut down to open up those new spaces? What about the wonderful roof, with its pool deck style chairs, where guys would lounge naked and smoke cigarettes in the warm summer night? But Grant seemed more interested in the private rooms, some of which had doors definitely closed, some had open doors with bodies in all states of preparation, while others had guys having sex for anyone who might be interested to watch. (Again, why bother with the porn?) Forest hoped that everybody was using PrEP and condoms (provided at every corner of the building, along with silicone lube, for those whose eyes were sharp enough to see them), but again, not the place for judging. But the real point of anxiety was being evaluated by lots of judgmental eyes, eager to detect whatever they regarded as a flaw. Forest knew that he was not a cover model for *Men's Fitness*, though all those hours at his gym did keep him in reasonable shape. Grant, of course, was on a different plane altogether.

As they walked, Forest knew that guys were staring at Grant. It was dark, but not so dark that Grant's looks went unnoticed. Even as Forest gave himself a stern little lecture about not overvaluing looks and the psychological damage done by exalting impossible standards of male beauty, he couldn't help smiling a bit to himself that he was here with such a hot guy. Good thing that Grant's greenness was not especially visible—though he wondered if anyone else would see it. He was becoming oddly protective of Grant; Forest worried that he might be subjected to serious gay shade if anyone discovered his little pigment issue. Admittedly, Grant never seemed to want or need protection, least of all from Forest. But his greenness had become an open secret between the two. They both knew of it (surely Grant knew, right?), but both chose not to say anything. They had a kind of vibe going—why ruin it?

Forest had not been paying attention at all to the scowling red numbers next to the porn movies. He didn't even know what room Grant had rented for them. But then Grant took his hand and said, "Let's go." As he stumbled along, he trusted that Grant would find his way in the endless dark hallways, lit only by occasional shafts of light from the open invitation or exhibitionist rooms.

Overthinking as usual, Forest wondered if this was more romantic than just going back to his place or Grant's. (What would Grant's apartment look like?) Couldn't Grant have saved himself a lot of money by just taking him home? But maybe something about the public nature of Sweatshop was a turn-on. It was a definite ego-boost to be here with Grant. He knew that some guys frowned on couples going to Sweatshop together. They were just washing their clean linen in public. But Forest was fairly sure that he and Grant were not exactly a couple—they were friends. Friends with benefits. Friends who had sex (or at least would have sex, since they hadn't done anything yet). As usual, Forest couldn't quite decide how he felt. But he did feel a bit of pride that the pandemic had not stopped gay sex. That was something of an achievement (to say nothing of monkeypox). And he liked the nonjudgmental attitude of

Sweatshop. Everybody knew why everybody else was there, and unity of purpose swept away a lot of posing and nonsense of gay bars (or straight ones, for that matter). And even if Grant ended up, as Forest feared, going home with someone else, at least Forest could know that he had had a moment.

Grant led Forest into their little room: not much more than a closet, it was as stark as Forest remembered. Like all the rooms in Sweatshop, it had no ceiling: the rooms were all open overhead—it was a cross between a cubicle and a cell. The walls were high, but you could definitely hear the sounds from next door—and presumably, you wanted to. A bed, a mirror, a tiny side table, and that was that. Grant turned to him. One of the big events in foreplay, removing clothes, was conveniently eliminated by Sweatshop standards. No worries about problematic zippers or shirt removal messing up carefully coiffed hair. But somehow, as he stood there with Grant in nothing but a towel, he felt even more awkward than he would have if he had to remove full Renaissance garb with cravats and pantaloons. Grant stared at him, and he stared back. Awkward pause. Should he make the first move? Should Grant? Forest defaulted to gazing soulfully into Grant's eyes, hoping that doing so would make him look as if he knew what was going on and what was going to happen. Grant smiled back at him. At Grant's smile, Forest wanted to dissolve into a puddle but just took a step closer.

At last, they came together in a long embrace. For some reason, Forest found himself focusing on the wonderful pine-y smell from Grant, as if he were in a deep wood and could smell the rich scent of the green needles. The thought crossed his mind that if he told anybody about this, they would ask if it was like hugging a bottle of Pine-Sol, so he thought he'd probably keep this impression to himself. And Grant's skin! Forest found his hands playing with Grant's chest hair, gently combing it with his hand and massaging it. He realized how much he had been missing skin-to-skin contact (which was never Ray's strong suit). He could feel his whole body relax as he got close (very close) to Grant.

With great patience, Grant slowly began a trail of kisses down Forest's body—his chin, neck, chest, and farther—until he at last came to a very stiff cock. Overthinking things as usual, Forest wondered if he should reach for a pillow from the bed. Wouldn't Grant's knees get hurt kneeling on the iffy floor of Sweatshop? Grant's tongue explored Forest with long sweeps, and Forest wondered if there were some way he would inconspicuously lean backward and reach for the pillow. Grant's mouth slowly closed over Forest and traveled down his length, while Forest tried stretching one arm gingerly toward the pillow but worried about dire consequences from any sudden movement. Grant expertly varied his speed and direction, and Forest was now fretting over Grant's beard, which had the potential to become very tickly when Grant went in really deep. Not to say that Forest was not enjoying the experience (a lot), but he seemed to have a talent for letting his thoughts travel to deeply irrelevant topics when his attention ought to be directed elsewhere.

He was gently swaying his hips in time with Grant's mouth. (The overthinking of the moment was worry if the sway was going to be a problem? Some guys preferred it if you just stood there. But Grant didn't seem to be objecting.) They were managing a beautiful, spontaneous celebration of male-male pleasure, accompanied by brief pauses for Grant to remove pesky strings of Forest's pubic hair from his mouth (accompanied by Forest's feeble chirps of "sorry").

Just as things began getting serious and Forest's attention was focused, a nasal voice announced, "Sorry guys. I'm in here for just a sec. One of the previous guys dropped his hearing aid in here. I'll be out as soon as I can." One of the twinks (how many of them were there?) who staffed Sweatshop darted in and started to move the bed away from the wall so that he could rummage along the floor. Forest had never lost an erection so fast. He and Grant separated. Even though Sweatshop was as public as anyone could ask, there was still something about being interrupted in the middle of oral sex that killed the mood faster than reruns of the *700 Club*.

Forest said to Grant, "We're outta here," and Grant's "Good idea" came back immediately. Forest was furious and stormed out in what used to be called "high dudgeon." Grant was right next to him and just kept his arm around him. Even though Forest said nothing, his thoughts were racing, as usual, in ways that kept his stress up. The nerve of that guy! Could he sue? Could they get their money back? Who loses a hearing aid at Sweatshop? But if younger guys got into older ones, then such things were likely to happen. But who decided that the Twink Brigade could invade at any second?

Slowly, as Forest regained his temper, Grant took over leading them. They found a wide, black staircase in a corner, and Grant led them down it in search of more privacy. A floor that was, if possible, even darker than the one that they had left was their next stop. Forest would usually use the flashlight app on his phone to find his way in such darkness, but the phone was locked up with his other valuables. Forest vaguely remembered that this had been where the BDSM equipment was kept: slings, St. Andrew's cross, implements that Forest was too clueless to know exactly how they worked. Forest never judged guys into leather, but he was so vanilla that he made vanilla look like Tabasco. But the floor seemed pretty deserted. Whereas the first floor of Sweatshop had been busy for an early hour, this floor was so quiet that Forest wondered if it was still in use. Could it have become something like a sex storeroom? Sweatshop must need storerooms like any other business. At least it was quiet.

Grant led him along, but it soon became clear that they were lost. The stairway that they had come down had disappeared—or at least they could not find it. Arm in arm, they roamed cluelessly. Forest had never spent much time in this section, and, even if he had, the redesign of the place had rendered it completely unfamiliar. His irritation at the twink's interruption was giving way to irritation at being lost in Sweatshop. This was not how this evening was supposed to go. Surely there would have to be a door or something nearby. When Grant muttered, "I think we're lost," Forest could think of nothing except, "Does this mean that the witch gets to eat us now?" He heard Grant chuckle softly. Grant thought Forest's jokes were funny! Ray the humorless had always stared stony-eyed at Forest.

Finally, after what seemed like an eternity of stumbling (about ten minutes), Forest saw a door that seemed to be painted sort of white. At least, it was much easier to see in the darkness than almost anything else. "Grant, see the door?"

"Let's do it." Grant still carried his towel at his side. Forest had his wrapped like a fig leaf. They both had had enough of meandering in the dark. It looked as if there might even be light on the other side of the door, though it was difficult to be sure in the prevailing gloom. It was time to get out of there.

As fast as they could, they went out… but not into Sweatshop. As the door clicked shut behind them, they found themselves outside in the side street next to Sweatshop, which used to be a glum, dark alley but had recently been gentrified into a twee gay bar (The Peach and Eggplant) and overpriced coffee shop. The coffee shop was closed, but the patrons waiting in the cold to get into the Peach and Eggplant erupted at the site of Grant:

"Way to take it off, Daddy!"

"We're here for it."

"I'm more here for it than he is."

"You're a cute couple except for him" (meaning, presumably, Forest).

"Can you be the marshals at our next Pride parade?"

"Green is the new black!"

"Can I take a selfie with you? It will go so viral on my Instagram."

And what felt like hundreds of cell phones began snapping pictures.

Grant turned to Forest, who now began to look as green as Grant, but for a different reason, and said, "This was not what I had in mind."

"Guess what? No door handle on this side."

"That is not possible."

But Forest was right. The door had no outside handle. They were stuck in the street during a Pine Rapids February, barely wearing towels, and furnishing the Peach and Eggplant with the cheapest and best show in town.

Just then, a blast of sound made their ears hurt. It was a loud, earsplitting peal of noise. "What idiot pulled the fire alarm switch?" Forest wondered. Had a cattle prod gotten out of control in one of the BDSM rooms? Had a violet wand backfired? Had some moron dropped a match trying to light a cigarette (did anyone even use matches anymore)? The noise was deafening. Even though Sweatshop was pretty closed in terms of windows, he saw guys beginning to stream from the entrance, pulling on their clothes, looking generally disheveled, accompanied by waves of adulation from the Peach and Eggplant, whose patrons began pouring out of the bar despite the cold to watch the show.

Then Forest heard someone screaming, "What asshole opened the fire emergency door?" Sweatshop's manager was tearing through the building, looking demented. He was standing to lose a huge wad of cash because that fire alarm had squelched a thousand erections. He screamed and screamed. Forest was sympathetic. Who could have been so stupid as to open one of those "alarm will sound" doors, the kind that caused occasional disruptions at his gym? Maybe some homophobe who thought messing with men having sex was a laugh riot.

Just then, Grant grabbed his shoulder: "I think that was us."

Forest stared: "Huh?" He was naked, in public, humiliated, and not in the mood for puzzles. Grant just looked at him. And then it hit Forest. The door to the street must have been the emergency exit. Forest immediately went on the defensive. It had been pitch-black. Of course they couldn't see that it was supposed to be an emergency exit.

Just then, the manager came outside and spotted them. "You two!" He pointed with all the fury of Uncle Sam Wanting You. "You two did this!" He had seen them on the club's video cameras, and his identification was unfortunately accurate.

The mob at the Peach and Eggplant cheered even more loudly:

"We love you forever."

"Heroes all."

"Out of the bathhouse and into the streets!"

"Would you host the next drag bingo?"

"Can we get you on the city council?"

Forest felt his stomach turn to ice, which matched the temperature. He and Grant were naked, freezing, and in trouble. Damn those video cameras! Heaven knows where they had been stashed because it could not have been darker in Sweatshop. If push came to shove, Forest was the one in trouble, not Grant, since he had opened the door. Though he knew he should run, he was too humiliated to move. He would have to go back inside, apologize to the manager, maybe pay a fine, get his clothes and stuff, and skulk home in a puddle of shame.

The manager was muscling his way through the crowd straight toward Grant and Forest. Grant whispered, "We have to get out of here. Fast," and began to walk away. Forest was going to tell him that the way he was walking just led to a dead end. They'd have to come back this way sooner or later. But when Grant saw that Forest was not following him, he ran back, grabbed Forest's hand, and started a serious run. Forest was grateful that they both had at least kept their shoes on, but their towel-fig leaves, which were none too sturdy, soon fell off their bodies, to the ecstasy of the Peach and Eggplant mob. Forest panted to keep up with Grant. His motivation was low because he knew that they were headed toward a brick wall at the end of the street.

They were quickly out of sight of both Sweatshop and the Peach and Eggplant. There was nothing on the street open at this hour, and no traffic because it was a dead end. It felt dark and creepy. Forest sensed Grant's grasp on his hand growing even tighter, so tight that it was almost painful, especially in his shoulder. And Forest noticed his feet feeling weird. They were no longer pushing against the ground. The familiar impact of sole of foot on pavement had faded, and Forest felt as if there was nothing for him to push. His running sped up, but he was not sure he was getting anywhere.

It was dark, so it took him a bit of time to register what was happening. He felt as if his feet were not pushing against anything for a simple reason. They were not pushing against anything. Grant was holding on to him tightly because Grant was not just ahead of him, he was also above him. It hit Forest that they had left the ground and were rising up. Not "up" as in "upstairs" or "up on the top shelf" but "up" as in "up into the air."

Grant had been holding Forest's right hand, but now he swung him up and hugged him closely, one arm around Forest's shoulders, the other around his lower back. Grant's body was warm, but the surrounding air was freezing. Forest held tight to him, though he did not feel secure. As what was happening slowly dawned on Forest, his body grew rigid with fear, and he dug his fingernails into Grant's flesh.

When he craned his neck, Forest saw, in the cold moonlight, two delicately luminescent sheets of what looked like fine emerald-green webbing sprouting from Grant's back. To call them "wings" was not right. Not bird wings (no feathers). Not plane wings (no metal). Nothing like butterfly or insect wings, either. They looked like intricately patterned lace if lace had the durability of steel. They also did not flutter back and forth but seemed to follow their own complicated logic of folding and unfolding, rolling and unrolling, at great speed. At times they worked symmetrically. At other times each seemed to have its own plan of action, twisting, bending, and folding with precision. Panicked as he was, Forest realized that Grant was having to work overtime to keep them both aloft. Even as he appreciated Grant's virtuoso display of strength, he prayed that his life did not depend on the strength of Grant's grip.

As they both rose higher and higher, I wish I could say that they joined in a passionate embrace, that Forest and Grant had delicious aerial sex as they soared through the starlit sky. How much would I give to describe two men in a tight embrace, freeing themselves from the confines of gravity? Alas, my allegiance to truth in narrative demands that I describe what actually happened:

Grant: "Sweetheart, if thou stoppest wriggling, this will be much safer for both of us."

Forest: "AAAAAAAAAAAAAAAGGGGGGGGHHHHH!!!!"

Grant: "I promise thou'rt okay. We'll be at my home soon."

Forest: "OH MY GOD. PUT ME THE FUCK DOWN."

Grant: "I'd better detour so that we're over a park or river."

Forest: "I'M SLIPPING!!! I CAN'T HOLD ON ANYMORE."

Grant: "Can't hold to me or to thy bladder? We're over Edgeside Park, so we're good. You don't need to hold on. I've got you."

Forest: "WHAT THE HELL IS GOING ON?"

Grant: "Thou shalt be down in just a second."

What should have been a wildly romantic flight over Pine Rapids was for Forest more frightening than midwestern cooking. He screamed and flailed like an extra about to be tromped by Godzilla, to say nothing of losing complete control of his bladder. If the crowd at the Peach and Eggplant had seen his antics, he would have finally become the viral TikTok that he had so often imagined. But strangely, no one seemed to notice that two stark-naked men were flying over the city.

Chapter 10

Driving home with the kid, Ray felt himself sweating. He realized that it would take an army to clean his linen shirt, and he knew his day was ruined. Strange noises were emerging from the back seat. Ray had no child's seat, and the whole non-kidnapping had happened so fast that it never occurred to him to buckle the kid in.

Which made the toddler very, very happy. In the space of about two minutes, the child sprawled over the back seat upside down, sideways, and diagonally, explored mats on the floor, pushed the dials and buttons on the sides of each seat (watching the window go up and down was so exciting that he spent almost fifteen seconds watching it), climbed from one seat to another, stood up to examine the back, and jumped up and down in place because, hey, that was fun too. His favorite move was flinging himself down headfirst on the back seat to see how much he would bounce. When he, not surprisingly, knocked his head on the seat belt after one of his flings, he howled like a demon.

At the howl, even Ray knew something was wrong, but was not about to stop the car. If he did, somebody might see him, and if he opened the door, the kid might get out. Already a sweaty mess, he was even more stressed than he had already been. "Shut up!" he screamed at the child, which produced the expected result. If an adult demonstrates a behavior, a child is certain to mimic it. The kid screamed fit to wake the dead plus all their relatives. Ray, worn to a frazzle, grabbed a miscellaneous file in the seat next to him and thrust it into the back seat. As he did so, papers went everywhere. Strangely, this quieted the kid down. Ray could finally focus on getting home.

Until… he heard strange crunching sounds from the back of the car. "Don't eat the paper!" he yelled in a panic.

This produced an outburst of giggles from the kid: "No eat papah!" repeated over and over and over. But the crunching continued. And then, Ray found himself under siege. "Mee-yah!" screamed the kid, and started hurling pieces of paper that he had crumbled up into balls: "Mee-yah! Mee-yah!" The balls were going everywhere. They hit Ray in the head (not hard) and landed all over the front seat. Ray could only imagine what his usually pristine back seat must look like now. He gritted his teeth: almost home, almost home.

After an eternity, he pulled into his parking space in the condo garage. Even though the kid was still chattering away ("Mee-yah! Mee-yah!"), Ray needed a moment to catch his breath. His apartment was unprepared for a child, he knew. But as the Quyre had said, it was only for two weeks. How much damage could the kid do? He could just sleep on the couch and watch TV. What about clothes? Well, he could just wear what he was wearing. And what would it eat? He'd have to eat what Ray ate. Did it still need a bottle? Probably not: looked too old.

His head buzzing with the effort at having to plan his life, Ray got out of the car and opened the door to the back seat. His eyes widened. Shreds of paper were everywhere, along with mud and leaves from the kid's boots and pants, streaks of snot, a branch or two (how had they gotten in?), and seemingly hundreds of wads of paper. The kid had been in the back seat for ten minutes max. It was not possible to cause so much damage so quickly. But there it was. As he bent over to get the kid out, Ray asked, "Mee-yah?"

The kid added helpfully, "Fall fum sky!" It took Ray a second, but he figured out that "mee-yah" was "meteor." He was in for a long two weeks. Ray grabbed the kid's wrist and hauled him out of the car.

In the distance between his car and the elevator, Ray discovered that he and the kid had different approaches to walking. Ray, dreading discovery, strode fast and kept his head down. The kid was in a new world, filled with cars, which he had only just learned to distinguish from trucks ("tucks"). Each one deserved inspection and comment. Some were big and some were small, some had interesting stickers, some had antennae that stuck out, some were easy to climb under and others were easy to climb on, some had mirrors on the side that you could bend if you pushed hard. He was in paradise exploring garage wonders.

Ray watched in dismay. Just getting to his condo was looking harder and harder. He marched over, unglued the kid from the side of a Subaru, and stormed to the elevator with the kid over his shoulder. The kid, of course, howled his head off, and Ray felt his stomach turn queasy. He was so distracted that he had no energy to notice what usually would have been his focus: the kid's muddy boots, his filthy jacket, his tear-and snot-stained face, and his unspeakable smell. He had been so fixated on the unlikelihood of kidnapping a child that now, when the child had more or less fallen into his lap, he was completely unprepared. "Just let me get to the condo without being seen," he said to himself, as if it would help.

In the elevator, he put the kid down, who quieted his howls. Ray positioned him at the back corner of the elevator. He went to the opposite corner, looked at him hard, said, "No talking. No talking," and put his hand over his mouth. With surprising obedience, the kid put his hand over his mouth. But if anyone walked into the elevator, it would be obvious that Ray and the kid were there together, and no one had ever seen Ray with a child before. It did not help that the kid's adventures with seat belts in Ray's car had left a prominent red welt on his forehead. Ray wished he had the time to think of something smart to do, but the best he could come up with was to cross to the bruised kid's corner and stand in front of him to block anyone who might come in from seeing.

For the moment, the kid seemed entranced by the motion of the elevator and did not say much. Ray tried to gauge from the elevator speed if someone else was likely to get on. They were going up from the garage. Usually people who were already in the building wanted to get down rather than go up, so he thought that all was going well. But right after floor 7, he felt the gravity change in the elevator, along with a telltale slowdown. Someone was getting on and would certainly notice the kid, whose picture would soon be plastered on every billboard in Pine Rapids.

Floor 8. The door stopped. The kid, who had been miraculously quiet, charged out of the doors as soon as they opened. Ray grabbed him by the sleeve of his coat and whooshed him back into the elevator as Mrs. Denison got on. Ray knew her by sight: a stout middle-aged woman with a bad perm and steel-gray eyes. You did not mess with her. They nodded and stated each other's names. That was the totality of their usual communication. They joined in the chilly silence that was Ray's tradition in the elevator. With forced casualness, Ray leaned back a little, doing his best to hide the kid. He glued his eyes to the numbers overhead, as if by watching them, he could make the elevator move faster.

And then, without warning, a loud "Hewwo!" broke the silence. Ray's eyes grew wide. The kid was on the floor peeking between Ray's legs. Mrs. Denison looked startled, then mystified. Her eyes quickly darted around the elevator to see where the voice came from. "Here," the kid cheerfully shouted.

"Oh, and there you are indeed!" said Mrs. Denison. "Look at you! What is your name?"

"Keggy!" said the kid, who then commenced a long and incomprehensible stream of syllables, among which Ray thought he heard "silly man," "mee-yah," and "ewevay" ("elevator"). Ray realized that the kid was sharing his version of the afternoon's events, but he was too petrified to comment or even to look. He stared into the distance as if a kid were not speaking from between his legs and as if standing in front of him was not at all suspicious. He also pondered what kind of parent would name a child "Keggy."

Heaven at last had mercy on Ray, as he thought, when they reached the 11th floor, his floor. As soon as the doors opened, he swept the kid into his arms, muttered something about "helping a friend out" to Mrs. Denison, and hurtled toward his condo. He unceremoniously dumped the kid on the floor and charged into the kitchen to get coffee because he needed all the help he could get. Sitting at the kitchen table, he, for the first time, confronted the reality of two weeks of life with the kid. Where would he sleep? What would he eat? Did Ray have to look after him every second?

Ray was going into his usual mode of ignoring problems until he heard strange noises from his living room. He shook himself out of his stupor and dashed into the room, where the kid had carefully arranged bottles of Chateau Chat Noir 2009 Pauillac, Premier Grand Cru, Chateau de Singe Grand VIN Pauillac 2012, Queen of Hearts Brut Green by Armand de Brignac, and a Dom Perignon Brut Champagne 2012 (with its scents of toasted brioche) in a loose line. He had also grabbed a large, expensive clay sphere, decorated with beautiful Navajo patterns, that Ray had acquired on his travels. "Bowing pins," the kid shrieked, and, stepping back a few feet from the bottles, rolled the sphere toward the bottles. The Queen of Hearts went down, and the kid shouted "Geeee!" (=green). It also did more than go down. As it went down, it crashed against the Chateau de Singe with enough impact to crack completely. The champagne spilled on the shimmering azure Persian wool and silk rug as the kid shouted happily, "Mess!" (the one word he pronounced perfectly).

Ray stormed over and swept the kid away from the impromptu bowling alley and screamed, "Don't touch my wine!" at the kid, who, as in the car, responded by howling louder. And then the kid's smell hit Ray like a wall, and his stomach lurched. The kid continued to howl as Ray dragged the child to his luxurious bathroom and, with a lot of resistance, peeled off his filthy coat, boots, and shirt. But nothing could have prepared him for the horror awaiting him when he, after much struggle, removed the pants. "Accident!" yelled the kid happily. Ray leaned over the toilet, lost whatever was in his stomach, and felt the room spin.

Oh my God, I'm going to have to give this kid a bath, Ray thought. He poured in his tub an entire bottle of Fleurette scented hand soap and grabbed as many of his Versace towels as possible. Desperately holding his breath, he mopped up the kid as best he could and dumped towel after towel into a pile of shame (thank heavens his condo had a laundry machine in his unit).

Surprisingly, the kid was happy in the bath. Ray had turned on the jacuzzi attachment, and the kid enjoyed watching the water swirl and swirl. Ray wanted to dump all the kid's clothes, including the boots, as well as the Versace towels, into the incinerator as soon as possible, but realized that the laundry setting for "extra tough stains" would be a safer bet. There was no way he could put the kid back in the clothes he had worn, at least in their current state. After the bath, the kid looked, if not clean, then at least cleaner. Ray hauled him out and marched him to his clothes closet. At other times, Ray took great pride in his Brunetto Caccini polo shirt, but he was desperate. Loosely buttoned, it managed to cover up the kid in a way that was presentable, if not elegant. Diapers, underwear, socks, and shoes would have to wait.

This was the kid's first time wearing a shirt that had buttons, so he enjoyed pulling them as hard as he could to see if he could yank them off (why else would they be on a shirt?). Exhausted, Ray dragged the kid to his couch, plopped him on it, turned on the TV, and found a show that he had never seen before, *Teletubbies*. The kid was obviously familiar with it and yelled out names: "Dipsy! Noo-noo!" Ray sat, drained.

And then, he had a horrific vision. On the TV, a child's face had been projected into the image of a sun so that creepy glowing rays extended everywhere from it. It resembled a primitive form of child sacrifice, in which children were set on fire to propitiate a fierce god. Ray could hardly look at it. And the kid noticed. "Baby sun scare Way! Baby sun scare Way!" he chanted. And since this seemed to be the funniest thing he had ever seen, he broke once again into torrents of laughter, so much so that he could hardly get his words out.

Ray was too exhausted to protest, too exhausted to move, too exhausted even to watch *Teletubbies*. Though he and the child had not eaten, though he was even filthier than the child before his bath, though he was not in luxurious pajamas or his lavender-scented sheets, he felt sleep coming whether he wanted it or not. He had always wondered if he could ever sleep without the soothing touch of his vicuna sleeping mask. And now he found out.

Chapter 11

GRANT'S HOME turned out to be close, in a residential area filled with beautiful homes. He had a small house on a cul-de-sac surrounded by forest. From the outside, it was not remarkable, at least from what Forest could tell at night, but the inside was different. If Forest's capacity for amazement had not been exhausted by his ride, he would have been stunned. The first floor was less a house than a huge, glowing grotto, complete with a mini-pond about the size of a jacuzzi in the middle. Blue-green radiated everywhere. Plants that could never grow in a real grotto covered this one: mosses, bushes, flowers, and grasses in every shade of color. Rather than having lamps or chandeliers, the room was lit by glowing embers that studded the grotto. Nothing that looked like a standard chair or sofa was to be found, but moss-covered rocks and logs were shaped into surprisingly comfortable places to sit and even lie down. Forest, at last beginning to calm himself, said, "Your interior designer should not have watched *The Little Mermaid* so many times."

"Let's get thee cleaned up," said Grant.

Lying in a heap on a mossy stone, Forest said, "I can take care of myself, thank you," asserting his manly independence after spending the last twenty minutes shrieking louder than Brunhilde. Grant pointed to the mini-pond. Forest stared: "Are you kidding? First, why do you have a pond in the middle of your living room? Second, how do I know it's safe? It could be totally infected with brain-eating bacteria."

Grant said, "Thou canst sit there smelling like dried piss or take a quick bath with me and feel better." That did the trick. Forest swallowed whatever was left of his pride after the evening he had had. He knew that Grant had some explaining to do and that his own sense of the world was about to undergo serious revision. But given a choice between a paradigm-shattering lecture on the supernatural and a warm bath, Forest made the right choice. The lecture could always come later. Plus, now that he was back on land, he could once again enjoy the sight of Grant's body, which did not get old. He saw that Grant's wingy things folded up neatly into his back before he hit the water.

The water was warm and soothing, and Forest felt himself relaxing, despite the strangeness of all that had just happened. Grant looked even hotter when he was wet. Maybe they would have sex after all. As Forest's heart rate began to calm down and he was able to take deep breaths, he said to Grant, "We need to talk."

"'Tis not that complicated. Fairies exist, and I'm a fairy."

What did one say to that? Forest paused before responding. "A fairy? As in Tinkerbell?"

Grant snapped, "Why do humans always go right to Tinkerbell! Thou canst not have known, but for fairies, the T-word is just about the harshest insult there is."

"Sorry—it was the first thing that came to mind. I didn't mean to upset you. I'm not sure how to say this because I like you a lot and what you did back there was amazing, but… fairies don't exist. You are a very, very handsome guy who happens to have some back implant that lets him fly. Why not tell me more about that?"

"Forest, all humans have seen fairies, so how canst thou know we do not exist? In English, you have the T-word and maybe Puck. But the djinns of Arabia, the lares and penates of Rome, the Mogwai of China, the silver-white yumboe of Senegal, the peris of Indonesia, the sidhes of Ireland (the people of the mounds), the curupira of the Yupi, the Menehune of Hawaii…."

Forest's eyes were glazing over: "So you are Fairypedia?"

"Ask me anything about fairies you want to know."

How many have dreamed of just such a question, an opportunity to draw back the veil on the mysteries of the world beyond humans? How many have longed to have such a moment, when knowledge of the supernatural was in their grasp? And at this moment of possibility, Forest drew a complete blank. The evening was so different from what he had expected that he was lost. Fairies were supposed to be like Tinkerbell and were not supposed to be hunky gay men in Pine Rapids. Pressed by Grant, the best he could come up with was this: "Fairies live in forests and caves and so on. They don't have swanky Jacuzzis in the middle of living rooms in Pine Rapids."

"They do now," said Grant.

"But what exactly is a fairy? What powers do you have? Can you do magic?"

"Less than thou mightst think. We call 'sailing' what thou callest 'flying,' and we all can sail, though it takes some time to master. When we sail, we become invisible to the human eye, except for some slip-ups that have led humans to believe that they were being invaded by beings from outer space. As it turns out, there are no UFOs, only careless fairies.

"We live much longer than humans, but we are not immortal. In terms of our powers, they are limited. We can't force humans to do anything against their will. But once a human has started any action, we can help it or get in the way, without the human ever knowing of our aid or hindrance. I can do a few small tricks, such as putting information on your phone without typing it in. But any Disney wicked queen can do much more than real fairies."

"But why?"

Grant looked confused. "Why what?"

Forest tried again: "Why not have your own world and leave people alone?"

"Some fairies do. But fairies who help humans get stronger. They can sail higher and longer. They stay healthy, sleep better, are more mobile, and have a better quality of life. Fairies who live apart don't do as well. They have a lot of fun laughing at those of us who live in cities with humans, but they never survive as long."

"So helping people is the fairy equivalent to a Mediterranean diet?"

"What's a Mediterranean diet?"

"I'll explain later. Tell me more."

"We also need exercise, just like you, though there are special adaptations for fairies. We eat and sleep like you. For reasons that I can explain later, Pine Rapids has become a hub for gay fairies, but not all fairies are gay or male."

"You said fairies help humans. But what if humans don't want fairy help? What if they just want to do something on their own?"

Grant explained, "Fairies like variety, so they tend not to help one person more than once. It's a momentary boost, not a stream of help. But I meant what I said before about wanting to help thy gym. I hope you'll let me try."

"If it means letting you sail around the gym completely invisible, you'll have to let me think about it. And how do I know that you won't decide to mess things up?"

Grant paused. "This is a little bit embarrassing to have to say, but fairies think that messing up human activity is funny. The most popular shows on FayTube are of humans struggling against fairy mischief."

(*FayTube?* Forest thought to himself.)

"We have separate channels for human cooking disasters, laundry disasters, sewing disasters, instructional disasters, DIY disasters, and on and on. There is even a channel just devoted to IKEA. Fairies have so much fun with IKEA. Don't tell anyone, but a member of the governing board of IKEA is a fairy."

Forest's brain was swimming. Having fun with IKEA disasters made sense, but everything else was hard to take in. Was he on some episode of *America's Funniest Home Videos* (was that show still on)*?* Or some video by one of those YouTubers or TikTokers who specialized in practical jokes? Now would be a great time for them to reveal themselves. He'd love to see how they taught Grant to do the flying (whoops, "sailing"), without some visible jetpack like the Rocketeer. Maybe if they revealed themselves, he could get on his knees and beg them to edit out the more embarrassing moments on his flight with Grant before the video made it to wherever it would be shown.

Yet the more Forest refused to believe what was happening, the more a part of him knew that he was not seeing things, not making things up, not the next viral TikTok sensation, with or without the embarrassing parts. Impossible as it was to believe, Grant had wings, which were actually quite beautiful. With those wings, he had flown, or sailed, him from Sweatshop. As Forest conjured up scenario after scenario, he realized that, in the end, the most probable explanation was that Grant was telling the truth: he was a fairy. Well, though Forest, remembering the end of *Some Like It Hot*, nobody's perfect.

He had started the evening worried about how to eat a gyro without looking like a slob and was discovering that everything he knew about the world had to be turned upside down. Why had Disney not done a better job of preparing him to cope with fairies? Fairies were real. Fairies interacted with humans all the time and could do magic. Pine Rapids was a hub of gay fairydom. But Grant still looked gorgeous, and he felt safe and warm. At some later time, he would overthink fairies in the way he overthought everything else. But now he knew he would need to get home, figure out how to retrieve his clothes, keys, and wallet from Sweatshop, feed Mothra (who would not be pleased that he was out so late), plan fitness classes, and on and on… but for better or worse, this was a special night. He couldn't waste it.

He and Grant talked and talked: about fairy sailing (fairies thought of themselves as air mariners, not pilots); justice (fairies who crossed the line from hindering humans to hurting them had their sailing license revoked); food (fairies loved saffron, custards, and flan); visibility (the weird green color rendered fairies mostly invisible to modes of detection, from eyeballs to radar, though they still had to be careful); jobs (some worked at human jobs; others at fairy-specific tasks like cleaning sails or training fairies to sail); there were fewer than two hundred in all Pine Rapids; fairies could die of old age; otherwise, many small shards of glass had to be embedded in their flesh to kill them, which happened rarely. Also, it turns out that the flying monkeys in *The Wizard of Oz* were supposed to have been gorgeous male fairies, but MGM got spooked at the last minute. Fairies still turned their backs to the screen during those scenes when they watched the movie.

In answer to some of Forest's questions, Grant also let him watch some fairy porn on the SpriteSex.com channel on FayTube. Forest thought he had seen everything that could be done in this genre, but this was a revelation. Wings, or sails, allowed whole new arrays of positions that Forest had never even contemplated. And there was evidently a way of stroking fairy sails that, done right, could bring a fairy right to the edge.

Exciting as all this was, it had been a much longer day than Forest had anticipated, and after a time, he could not keep his eyes open. The evening was catching up to him: nervous preparation, dinner, Sweatshop, the street, angry manager, flight, Grant's grotto/living room, the bath, and *Fairies for Dummies*. He had been hoping for long-awaited wild sex with Grant and was now falling asleep in the middle of his sentences. Grant walked to where Forest was and, with a few quick gestures, turned Forest's stone chair into a bed of thick moss. Forest thought that he had never had a mattress so comfortable. Yawning, he stretched himself out and, almost without knowing what he was saying, croaked out "Good night, sweetheart." Grant gently blanketed Forest and turned down the glow so that Forest would have complete darkness. He and Forest still had not had sex. But as Grant tiptoed away from Forest, he smiled and looked as happy as a puppy in springtime.

Late as it had been for Forest when, worn about by fairy trivia, he passed out, he woke up as always at 6:15 a.m. to get to work. He always marveled in fiction how, as soon as the supernatural appeared, characters' everyday concerns vanished, as if the bills could be paid, the cat fed, the dishes washed, all by themselves. That was not what real life was like. Fairies or not, Forest had a job to do, and if he did not get to Mothra soon, there would be signs of high displeasure next to which a slugfest with the actual Godzilla would be nothing. Groggy, he crawled out of the moss bed. Grant had put out a change of clothes for him, and they happened to be in his size. (Grant was a few inches taller.) Forest was expecting fairy clothes to be glittery and shiny a la '70s polyester, but they were super comfortable. And was Grant cooking? Something smelled amazing. He walked out of the grotto toward the alluring smells.

Forest was a little disappointed to discover that Grant's kitchen actually looked like a kitchen. He had been half hoping for a fairy remix of "Be Our Guest" from *Beauty and the Beast*. But the chocolate chip pancakes Grant had made quickly overcame any disappointment.

"If the way to a man's heart is through his stomach, you're there." Grant winked.

Forest took a deep breath and asked Grant, "The fairy thing is amazing. But beyond that, you're gorgeous, and a million guys, fairies or not, must be falling over themselves to get to you. Why me?"

Grant answered, "Good question. Thou'rt funny, cute, can sustain a conversation, art curious, and I love when we're together."

Forest nodded solemnly. "Don't let me stop you. Keep going."

Grant smiled, then reached over, took his hand, and said with more seriousness than Forest was expecting, "When most humans find out that I'm a fairy, they immediately beg me to get something for them. Thou would'st be amazed what humans ask for. One could not be convinced that I could not get him a longer member. They think that I am like the genie in *Aladdin*, and I'm not. Thou'rt the first man in a long time who has not asked for anything."

Forest was taken aback. What Grant said was true. Even though he had just found out that Grant was a fairy, he had never thought about trying to exploit him. Grant was such a knockout that that was enough. The fairy stuff was fun, as long as he was not hundreds of feet in the air, but not why he liked Grant. But now he started to second-guess himself.

Maybe he should have asked Grant for something? Was he just being stupid? But the more he thought about it, trying to exploit Grant seemed such a bad move that he had trouble imagining himself doing it. He was genuinely caught off guard. He had been detected in a good deed of omission of which he, Mr. Overthinking Champion, was unaware.

"But while we're speaking of it, even though thou hast not asked for anything, I have something to offer thee."

"I'll bet you do," said Forest, hoping that Grant might renew what had been interrupted the night before.

"Our time last night was interrupted. I hope we can resume soon?"

Forest said jokingly, "Believe me when I say I want to. But I'm going to have to get to work this morning. How about I give you a signal? If you ever hear me calling loudly for lube, that means I'm ready."

Grant smiled. "Noted. I'll be prepared since I am more than eager. But I wanted to ask thee about something else. Fairies are desperate to learn to swim. They can swim alongside humans only if they hide their sails. If they swim like fairies—diving in and out of the water with their sails aloft—the patterns on the water that they created make humans suspicious. In some cases, they fear that the fairy patterns are evidence of a UFO. In other cases, like the Loch Ness monster, fairy waves have been horribly misinterpreted. So fairies shy away from practicing water maneuvers because they upset humans too much. But thy pool would be perfect, if there could be a time when only fairies would be able to use it."

Forest was intrigued by the idea. They had women-only yoga, so why not fairies-only water fitness? Just watching Grant's sails twist and turn was a turn-on. And his gym needed new members. If Grant and his buddies could get him ten or twelve new members, he'd be in better shape to survive the damage of Grayson's. It also could be fun to adapt his water classes to the needs of fairies. Though he did not know fairy physiology or biochemistry, he did know how to teach fitness and hoped that the fairies would like him.

"Let's do it!" said Forest. "The gym opens at 6:00 a.m. Let's say 4:30-5:30 a.m. It's super early, but that's the best I can offer to guarantee some privacy for you all. Can we start next Tuesday?"

"Forest, this is huge! The fairies will be so excited!"

Chapter 12

"So, you sailed him back to your house … and then?" said JX.

"Naked, right?" added Tren.

"I want deets. Especially embarrassing ones. Hairy or smooth? Any tattoos? Does he moan? I hope he moans."

"How many times in an evening?" asked Tren, as if he planned to enter the answer into a spreadsheet.

"Enough, both of you!" exploded Grant. "This is not why I have asked you here. I have grave concerns."

JX turned to Tren: "Grave concerns! Sounds promising."

Tren sighed. "I have concerns, too. You never know with humans. Tried a relationship with a human. Seemed like dream daddy: tall, dad bod, white hair—balding a little, warm smile. But all he could talk about was his prostate."

"And back pain? They're never happy unless they're complaining about lumbar spines."

"Plantar fasciitis," Tren said. "And he had to be in bed by 9:30. I thought that was just for an afternoon nap, but no."

"If you want daddies, you have to be ready for the whole package, Cialis and all."

"The package wasn't the problem."

"Ah, I see … uncertain delivery date?"

"Body clocks not in sync."

Grant interrupted: "Tren, why art thou talking about bawdy clocks? What is a bawdy clock, anyway?" JX unsuccessfully restrained snickering.

Ignoring these reactions, Grant continued, "I need you both to come with me now."

"If you think that you are going to get out of telling us about your date, you are so wrong," said JX, almost composing himself.

Grant met the comment with silence.

Sighing, JX said, "Show us the way, O Fearless Fairy Leader. I'd call you 'FF' for short, but it might give others the wrong idea."

They were in Grant's grotto/living room, but he walked them to his study, a small room of glistening green. It was furnished in exquisite fairy taste. If the living room looked like an underwater grotto, this was a forest nook, with skilled interweaving of yellow broom, wild thyme, musk roses, and strategically placed condoms. Grant invited his friends to get comfortable on what looked like stools but were actually forest stumps. But before they did so, Grant lowered the blinds on the room's windows, blocking any view from outside. At this, they all removed their shirts. Their sails, as they called them, unfurled from their backs in beautiful colors, and they all looked relieved.

"The older I get, the harder it is to keep the boys tucked in without getting cramps," said JX. "Who needs plantar fasciitis with sails like these?"

Tren stretched and sat on one of the stumps. JX eyed a stump but remained standing. He said, "Our distant ancestors may have been comfortable with dead trees, but my sensitive tuchus…" Before JX could finish, Grant plopped a pillow adorned with a picture of a young Rupert Everett as Oberon on one of the stumps, and JX suddenly seemed much happier knowing he could sit on "divine Rupee."

Tren, out of the blue, channeled Miss Prism: "The chapter on the Fall of the Rupee you may omit. Even these metallic problems have their melodramatic side."

"What art thou talking about?" asked Grant, baffled, at which JX and Tren exchanged glances.

JX added, "Sorry, dear. I keep forgetting that Oscar was a bit after your time. And no one understands Wilde until they've made love to a severed head. 'I have kissed thy mouth, Jokanaan…' That was back when humans still had real creativity about sex." When Grant's eyes bulged wide, the usually restrained Tren smirked, and JX, cackling, almost fell off his pillow.

"Enough, both of you. I need you to be serious."

"Because?" said Tren.

"When thou art as old as I am…"

"Can't you just say 'well preserved'?" asked JX, who, though not as old as Grant, had been around for a few more centuries than he would admit to.

"That sounds like a gourmet pickle," commented Tren.

"I've been called worse," said JX.

"STOP," yelled Grant. "And, so thou know'st, 'Rupee,' as thou nam'st him, is far more appealing than the real Oberon ever was."

"The problem?" asked Tren.

"Bad teeth and worse odor."

"Cringe," said Tren.

"*Tres* cringe," added JX.

"No wonder Titania dumped him," added Tren.

"For Peaseblossom, too!" noted JX.

"Never understood why," said Tren.

"He blossomed where it counted."

"Aha. Makes sense."

"There's much more to be said about that story, but that is not why I asked you here," said Grant.

"You still haven't told us much about your night with Forest," said Tren.

"And I shall not because we have something of greater importance to accomplish."

"Comment on bad fashion choices?" asked JX. "Review the wreckage that humans call gardens in Pine Rapids?"

While JX nattered on about evil clumps of phlox and goldenrod that did not live up to its promising name, Grant reached behind some of the room's foliage and drew out what looked like a crystal ball—except that it stood on two stork-like legs and wore tiny sandals.

"Ooooh, new footwear!" said JX.

Grant said, "Hermès Chypre."

"You never go wrong with Hermès," said JX.

"Just bankrupt," added Tren.

Ignoring them, Grant placed the two-footed ball in the middle of the room and sat on a stump so that the three surrounded the ball. Quietly, in a rich baritone, he began humming a strange drone-like melody that sounded like a mashup of Donna Summer and Gregorian chant. The others joined in, Tren in a light tenor and JX in a flute-like falsetto. As they sang, their sails moved in time to the music in a fluttery dance, and it was hard to tell if the music drove the sails or vice versa. The glowing ball, the shimmering patterns of fairy sails, and the harmonies of the music created a mesmerizing spectacle.

"We're soooo pretty," cooed JX.

"Oh, Mary, it takes a fairy to make something pretty," quoted Grant.

JX and Tren looked at each other, eyebrows raised.

"*Boys in the Band*," said Tren. "Now required reading in fairy kindergarten."

"It's about time. And Grant is never as clueless as he looks," said JX. "I like that in a man. Sometimes."

"Concentrate!" hissed Grant.

The three resumed their chanting and fluttering. As they did so, the sandaled feet on the crystal ball moved as well, though not always in time to the music. The ball gyrated, twisted, leaned, and crossed, forward and back, side to side. At times, it looked like 70s disco; at others, like a big Bollywood production number; and at others, like the Nicholas Brothers at their most acrobatic. As it danced, the clear color with which it started gave way to a spectrum of other colors and patterns. Gradually, as the dance went on, one color predominated: orange. A fierce orange that looked both brilliant and angry.

One by one, the three fairies saw the orange in the ball's patterns. As they did so, their song faltered, their sails slowed down and stopped, and their chatter faded. They looked at each other, as if afraid to say what they were thinking. Even after they stopped, the ball's orange illuminated the room, jarring against the green of Grant's walls and the forest interior. Looking at the two colors clashing was so painful that the fairies had to close their eyes.

Quietly, JX murmured a chant, and Grant and Tren joined in after a few lines:

> *Orange and green, orange and green*
> *Fatal to fairies whenever they're seen.*
> *Orange and green, orange and green,*
> *Danger and death and nothing between.*
>
> *Green and orange, green and orange*
> *No rhymes for "orange," so there you're stuck.*
> *Green and orange, green and orange,*
> *Sure sign for fairies that all is amok.*

They sat in silence for a bit.

"But what is amok?" asked Tren. "Pine Rapids is as quiet as I've ever seen it. It makes Mayberry R.F.D. look like Gettysburg."

"What would be truly frightening for fairies?" said Grant.

"The return of bell bottoms?" suggested JX. "Heavy bangs? A rebranding of Tiger's Milk? A sudden trend for British mushy peas?" Tren shuddered.

The conversation stopped as the fairies, turning increasingly ashen, brooded on possibilities so scary as to be unmentionable. Their sails, which had danced so beautifully, drooped.

Finally, Grant whispered, "The Rite?"

JX and Tren gasped.

"You can't be serious. That's immmmpossible," said JX, drawing out the "m."

"Seems unlikely," said Tren.

"Who would do such a thing?" asked JX.

"I know not," answered Grant. "But the ball is never wrong, and that color meaneth that trouble is ahead."

JX and Tren glanced at each other, and their sails quivered. Much as they wanted to pretend that the ball was not orange, they could not deny what had happened. And as they knew, fairies never, ever mixed green and orange. As long as they could remember, it was a sign of catastrophe, like a rising sun for vampires or a plummeting graph for stockbrokers.

"What can we do?" Tren asked Grant.

"Prepare," he answered.

"Like Boy Scouts!" said JX. "Be prepared!"

"The who?" asked Grant.

"Never mind," said Tren. "What do you have in mind?"

"We need to defend ourselves and the way of life we have built in Pine Rapids. True, Pine Rapids may not be the most exciting town on the planet, but fairies have flourished and been happy here. I'm not willing to let that be destroyed without a fight."

"The last fairy army disbanded centuries ago. The fairies of Pine Rapids have no defensive training—except for the ones who do karate because they think the uniforms are cute. Any real threat would reduce them to a heap of lime Jell-O," said JX.

"So, we train."

"How much time do we have?" asked Tren, folding his sails back into himself and putting on his shirt.

"I know not. Something is better than nothing."

"And what does something involve?" asked JX, also folding up his sails and reluctantly getting dressed.

"My human, as you know, has a name, Forest, and a gym, Forest's Fitness. And it has a pool. As he said, he has offered to let us have fairies-only exercise classes in the pool before his gym opens to humans."

"Will I have to get wet?" asked JX.

The other two stared at him.

"Do you know what chlorine does to skin?"

"We shall begin lessons with Forest on the morrow."

JX began to say something, and Grant cut him short: "No exceptions. I will send an announcement on *FayLine, CNN: Nixie,* and *State of the Brownie.* What else would you suggest?"

"No young fairies watch news. Reach them some other way. Something catchy on PuckPock," said Tren.

"Canst thou do that for me?" Grant asked. "We need to get the word out fast." Tren nodded.

"How exactly is this going to work? I doubt Forest, however gifted he may be in other areas, will know how to train fairy defenses," said JX.

"Defense is coordination. In Forest's class, we shall become stronger, faster, and more coordinated. Then I can adapt his training to defense. We will sail in formation, learn how to counter the enemy, and practice dodging flying glass."

The words "flying glass" hung in the air as the three fairies looked at each other.

"Can't we just do this ourselves in some field or other?" whined JX.

"Too dangerous. If our invisibility failed for an instant, we would be seen. Forest's gym gives us a space where we can be safe. We will be neither seen nor interrupted. And fairies learn quickly."

Tren nodded, but JX still looked sad. "I'll have to get up early. It will be cold and wet. I'll have to exercise. It sounds miserable. Beyond miserable."

Grant said, "Imagine a room filled with hot male fairies in their Speedos."

"I'll be there first thing," said JX.

CHAPTER 13

FAR TOO early on a cold February Tuesday, Forest confronted a rowdy mob of fairies in his gym's pool. He had hoped for ten to twelve new members. Grant had gotten him almost seventy. For once, he decided not to worry about a lifeguard. It was hard enough to get a guard under regular circumstances, much less with supernatural beings. Although the fairies' ages varied, being in the pool reduced their collective mental age to about seven. And they were having a full-on fairy fiesta. Until this morning, Forest had seen only Grant, though he had also met Tren and JX, who were all part of this early-morning crowd. But now he faced an explosion of greenish torsos, some in as good a shape as Grant; others, not so dazzling. According to Grant, most were gay, but there were even straight fairies in the mix. JX and Tren, who were there, gave him a few quick pointers about what they called "faydar," their ability to figure out without asking which fairies were gay and which were straight. Beautifully maintained sails were a big clue.

As Forest watched them, gay or straight hardly seemed to matter next to the sheer fun of playing in the water in a way that fairies rarely could. They were splashing, sailing high above the water, diving, soaring, creating mini-whirlpools, imitating flying fish, building monster waves, and competing with each other for who could zoom underwater the fastest. Forest's class plan was not going to be much help with this crowd. They barely even noticed that he existed because they were having so much fun on their own. Forest was playing disco for them, but he soon found out that they would rather listen to fairy divas: Pixie Houston, Lady Kelpie, Dolly Peri, Aretha Fairy, and many others. He promised to get their music for next time.

After about twenty minutes of random water chaos, Forest was watching a group of three fairies practicing what looked like synchronized sailing: a combination of swimming, sailing, and diving in which all three tried the same moves at the same time. That was it! Forest went over to them, introduced himself (they had all heard about him through Grant, who had made sure to include the most embarrassing details in everything he said about Forest), and suggested some other moves that they might want to try. They were game, and soon Forest had them adapting a whole array of water exercise moves to fairy skills: syncopated cross-country skis, helicopters, hacky sacks, rockets, and more. The fairies, especially the gay ones, loved combining exercise with the choreography and had a blast. They had invented fairy rhythmic gymnastics for the water.

As the other fairies saw what Forest and his group were doing, they wanted in on the action because this party was too good to miss. Although Forest was used to teaching people who stayed in the water, he had been a fitness instructor long enough to be flexible. He had them practice moves high out of the water, just above the water, and deep in the water, moves forward and back, side to side, and twisting. The fairies loved rapid transitions from one level to another, which usually involved them colliding with each other, accompanied by fairy invective:

"Fat gremlin!"

"Out of the way, Miss Imp."

"Do us a favor and shave: way too much SHF (scary hairy fairy)."

"Girlfriend, this hob is a blob."

"You make trolls look glamorous."

And, Forest noted, plentiful use of the T-word as a friendly insult.

At about 5:15 a.m., with the fairies in full chaos of their workout party, Tren, who had stepped out for a moment, came tearing back into the pool. He had been so reserved when Forest had first met him that Forest was unnerved by how upset he seemed to be. For the first time all morning, the other fairies quieted when they saw Tren's face.

"Grant, out of pool now and come."

"What is it? Thou seem'st upset."

"NOW." Grant quickly sailed out of the pool and went with Tren.

As soon as Grant and Tren left, the other fairies, who had restrained themselves for the five seconds of the dialogue, burst out into a volley of chatter. They all wanted to see what had so upset Tren and flew out of the pool to follow him. A huge mass of dripping-wet fairies, smelling of chlorine, stood congregated in the not-especially-large front lobby of Forest's gym.

"Look!" one of them yelped as he pointed to the street.

It was still dark outside, so Forest could not see much. But as he peered more closely, he could see something that unnerved him. Odd horselike forms were galloping through the street. Impossibly, instead of running on all fours, they were on their hind feet so that their movements blurred human and animal. Snow-white with eyes burning like red coals, they generated sparks from their hooves and even out of their eyes. For Forest, the sparks were the easiest part to see. The rest was a blur, but the fairies could obviously see more plainly than he could. Few humans seemed to know what was happening, maybe because most of them were still asleep.

The chatty fairies fell silent as they watched these spectral horses gallop through the street. When Forest turned to Grant for an explanation, he was stunned to see just how upset Grant was. He was usually so in control, so on top of things. But not now. His tan skin, with its greenish highlights, was ashy pale. His eyes were wide, and he was sweating. Not knowing what else to do, Forest went to him, caressed his forearm, and said, "It's okay. It's going to be okay."

As soon as he did so, the fairies around him burst into chatter—but not chatter that Forest could follow because they were talking in Fay, the fairy language that he suddenly realized was what Tren and JX had been speaking when he first met them in the coffee shop. Forest assumed that they were talking about the specters, but he did not care. His focus was Grant. Forest was usually the upset and uptight one, but now roles were switched (did that make him verse? Forest wondered). Grant was an emotional mess, while Forest was able to be strong and comforting, largely because he had no idea what was going on. It had been a long time since Forest could support a boyfriend, since Ray, Sir Snow Queen, had never stooped to show emotion. As Forest stood next to Grant, he suspected that anything that upset fairies this much was probably not good for people either. But for now, he'd wait until Grant was ready to talk.

After a bit, Grant sighed, "I can't believe I'm having to tell thee this. This is the sort of thing that fairies never imagine humans learning."

"What can I say? I'm a lucky guy."

"Wait till thou hast found out what's going on, then decide. Thou mayst not feel so lucky. I think I'm going to need thy help even more than before."

"Of course," Forest said, flattered that Grant thought to consult him.

"I need to do what humans call brainstorming with thee."

"Okay. I can brainstorm. A heads-up that the gym is going to open soon, so the fairies will need to put on their public faces."

Grant turned to the fairies in the lobby and gave a short speech in Fay. They understood and quickly moved to the locker rooms to dress and move along.

Forest and Grant also cleaned themselves up in the locker rooms and then reassembled in Forest's office. There, Grant explained:

"Those horse-shapes, called 'the graunt' though they have no connection to me, are a fairy warning system. Traditionally, they appear before a major fire. Humans could not see the ghost horses, but they could see the sparks and hear dogs barking at them. The barking wakened humans, who were then better able to manage the fire. Yet as times had changed and human alarm systems had improved, the graunt's purpose had shifted. It was now less about fire than impending danger more broadly."

JX, who had evidently overheard them, added, with the enthusiasm of an archivist: "Don't listen to him. He knows nothing about it. Now listen, y'all, because I'm taking 'Fairy History' for $5,000. The graunt is among the oldest of fairy traditions. I know, it does sound a little like 'grant,' but it has nothing to do with His Fairy Hotness. The phenomenon is even mentioned by Gervase of Tilbury in his great *Otia Imperialia*. Joseph Ritson, the brilliant compiler of fairy lore, describes it when he says that it 'very often appears in the streets, in the very heat of the day or about sunset, and as often as it makes its appearance, portends that there is about to be a fire in that city or town. When, therefore, in the following day or night, the danger is urgent, in the streets, running to and fro, it provokes the dogs to bark and, while it pretends flight, invites them, following, to pursue, in the vain hope of overtaking it. This kind of illusion creates caution to the watchmen who have the custody of fire, and so the officious race of demons, while they terrify the beholders, are wont to secure the ignorant by their arrival.'"

Forest's eyes were beginning to glaze over at JX's fairy TED Talk. "So is there supposed to be a fire? And it's not the heat of the day nor a sunset."

JX said, "True, but Ritson is sometimes a wee bit shaky on the details. He writes 'grant' for 'graunt,' for example. But, honey, we can't expect humans to get everything right about fairies. Where would we boys be without a bit of mystery?"

Grant cut in: "Forest, I need thee to understand how serious this is. Thou are right that the graunt were not warning about a fire. It is much, much worse. They were warning about a child."

"A child?" asked Forest, who had not seen that coming.

"A human one, not fairy," JX added.

Forest thought of the children that he knew, mostly kids of his employees. Could any of them be in danger? Why would fairies care about a human child?

Somewhere in the back of his memory, Forest remembered that fairies were supposed to steal human children and substitute fairy children for them. They were called "changings" or "changelings" or something like that. But no fairies he had met showed the least interest in children. Nor had Grant ever mentioned any connection between fairies and kids, so Forest felt lost.

"The only threat I can imagine that fairies would pose to human kids is that they might accidentally land on top of them. But otherwise?"

Grant sighed. "It's about magic."

"But you guys don't do magic. You told me that you couldn't do magic, just help or hinder humans in what they were already doing."

"Just because we don't doesn't mean we can't, at least in the right circumstances. Even though fairies are not born with dark magic, they can earn it. To get the most powerful magic, fairies need the blood sacrifice of a human child. Such a sacrifice would give the fairies responsible for it the power to bend any fairy or human to their will. In no time, they would dominate every aspect of fairy life."

"Okay, so fairies have a possible if messy path to magic. What does this have to do with anything?"

"Oh, honey, if you only knew," murmured JX. "Grant, you had better tell him."

Grant went on: "Hundreds of years ago, ambitious fairies known as the Quyre were desperate for power. They found a child, made the sacrifice, and reduced the fairy world to misery. Fairies who had been free, happy, and independent became slaves. The wretchedness stopped only when the inevitable occurred."

"The networks canceled their reality show?" asked Forest.

JX giggled, and Grant even smirked for a second but soon turned serious. "No, they turned on each other. Having murdered a child to get magic, they murdered to keep it. One by one, the Quyre eliminated each other, each time in a hail of flying glass. Soon, the entire Quyre was dead, with nothing to show for their effort except skin shining with shards.”

“It's just like *Treasure of the Sierra Madre*, except with less Humphrey Bogart!”

“Oooh, good answer,” said JX.

“What's *Treasure of the Sierra Madre*?” Grant asked cluelessly.

“I'll explain later. Go on with the story,” said Forest.

“After the catastrophe, fairies agreed to put dark magic behind them. Whatever it might gain was not worth the havoc that it caused. In the Brownie Ban, under pain of immediate execution, fairies were not to kidnap human children for any reason. While there were inevitable interpersonal feuds and rivalries among fairies, they had lived peacefully enough for hundreds of years. There had never again been the slavery that had been so hard for all fairykind during the magic years.

“But all that has just changed. The appearance of the graunt was a warning that meant that someone or group of someones had broken the Brownie Ban. Fairies are planning to kidnap and murder a human child, and it will happen in Pine Rapids. A child is in danger, but has not yet been sacrificed. We need to find it before anything happens.”

“We?” Forest squeaked. “You mean you and other fairies, right?”

“Oh, darling, you are so in the middle of this,” said JX.

“Forest, I am a local leader to the fairies. To humans, Pine Rapids does not mean much, but to fairies, it is one of their hubs. Fairies here will look to me in a crisis, and they will look to thee because they know that we are seeing each other.”

Do they know that we still haven't had sex? thought Forest, keeping his curiosity to himself.

“And that's where I need thy help. To make sure that nothing like the violence of the past ever occurs, fairies have kept their distance from human children. They know nothing about them. Please help us.”

“But if you haven't noticed, I'm a gym owner, not an early childhood specialist. What makes you think I know anything about kids either?”

“Where would be the easiest place in Pine Rapids to kidnap a child?”

Forest thought for a moment. “Maybe a preschool?”

Grant's eyes grew wide: “What's preschool?”

"You don't know?" (Grant was right. Fairies did not know much about children.) "It's a school for very young children to prepare them for elementary school."

"Of course! Forest, thou'rt brilliant! I must run and inform the others. JX, come with me."

Grant ran out of the lobby. Forest wanted to follow him but had to stay and look after his gym. Besides, he was not sure he could help. Sex with Grant was now looking farther off than ever. Sweatshop had been a catastrophe, and the revelation of Fairy had been a lot for Forest to process. Grant had not pressed him, even though Forest was more than ready to be pressed. But now, Forest could tell, Grant's energies would be channeled to coping with this new threat. Though he had no official titles, Grant was the leader of the local fairy community. The fairies looked to him, and the pressure was on. But at least he wanted Forest's help.

CHAPTER 14

As Ray had predicted, in four days, the abduction of Craig Wallace from Kali Montessori was everywhere. The truth of the graunt's warning had been confirmed before the fairies had even started looking for a child. As soon as the story broke, Grant became obsessed. He read every newspaper article, scoured human and fairy social media, and glued himself to local reporting. Although Forest would have loved to talk about anything else, Grant had time for this child alone. Forest was not as certain as Grant that fairies had abducted him, but he understood that the whole affair was a calamity for the fairy community. And so, in Grant's house, they found themselves watching the 5:00 p.m. local news with the inevitable Linda Dahlquist, local reporter and premature blond, giving the latest details.

Most of what she said was familiar, but she did add a new twist: "Although it was first reported that Craigy Wallace was taken from his preschool, the police understand that Craigy was taken after school, once all the children had been dismissed. He was kidnapped somewhere in the few blocks between the school and his house. The police are now focusing on Craigy's home life. His parents have separated, and he allegedly lives with his father. But that father, although he owns a house in Pine Rapids"—image of dismal house with weedy, overgrown yard—"has no settled address. We have not been able to contact him. From what we at channel KMSC have been able to determine, neighbors look after Craigy. And now let's go to Kristin Robinson, who is interviewing one of these neighbors, Madalyn Mulcahy."

Forest turned to Grant, listening as if his life depended on what Madalyn Mulcahy would say. It turned out to be not much more than that Craigy was a fun boy who did not mind being shuttled from house to house.

"Poor kid," said Forest. "He's lucky the neighbors pitch in."

"Is this not how all humans raise their children?"

"Um… no. Do fairies even have parents?"

"Hast thou seen *Invasion of the Body Snatchers*?"

"Of course, but the fact that you ask makes me nervous."

"It's such a great sci-fi flick from the 50s about mindless conformity, fear of takeover, paranoia, and the claustrophobia of small towns."

"You know it's been remade? But never mind that. You're telling me this because…?"

"Because aliens in the movie are born from pods. Like huge pea pods. They grow in them. Believe it or not, that's a lot like how fairies are born."

"I'll bet you were a cute pod."

"Pod fetishism is big in fairy porn (I can show thee clips on FayTube), but it's not my thing."

"So you're pods, but not actual body snatchers. Each pod is a separate fairy, right?"

"Exactly. When the pod is ripe, the fairy hatches, looking like a full-fledged adult, but ignorant about the world that they live in. So their childhood is not about physical maturation but about understanding the world. Tren is only about six years since hatching. JX is much older."

"I have images of fairies emerging from weird pod shapes, like *Aliens* with less blood—"

(Which produced the expected "What's *Aliens*?" from Grant.)

"Thanks for those nightmares. That may be all I can handle right now. Do unpodded fairies go to fairy school?"

"In the old days, they did. There were legendary schools: Flyover, Spriton, Brownieminster, Kelpie on Troll. But now it's mostly online training. Tuition became too expensive. Particular fairies mentor the young and help them. When I'm not worrying about the graunt and trying to romance my hot boyfriend (I see you're blushing), I'm a sailing instructor because sailing gives newly hatched fairies the most trouble." Forest blushed at the part about himself.

"Fairies must be VERY happy when they find out that you will be their teacher. And tell me more about your hot boyfriend."

"I could tell thee stories…" Forest sat up eagerly. "But I need to get back to the child. If he has indeed been kidnapped and becomes a sacrifice, the Apixielypse is on us. But who would take a child for such a purpose?"

Forest grinned at "Apixielypse," assuming it was a joke, but one look at Grant's grim face convinced him that, ridiculous as the word sounded, Grant was serious. Forest squelched his smile.

Grant looked up at Forest and expected him to make some pronouncements about the kidnapper. Forest stared blankly and then said randomly, "Maybe it was somebody who did not have to work at the time of the kidnapping and who had a getaway car. But that doesn't take us far."

Forest racked his brains to help Grant but finally realized that looking for the kidnapper was a dead end. He asked instead, "Where is this sacrifice going to happen?"

"We call it the Rite, the final stage in a fairy's access to black magic. It could be anywhere, but historically, it's been a great solemnity, with hundreds invited to watch. I believe that those who are planning have pride big enough to want their Rite to rival what humans think of as the Superbowl halftime."

"Okay. That's helpful," said Forest, surprised at what Grant did and did not know about human culture. "The Superbowl doesn't just happen and definitely not in secret. It requires zillions of people and lots of money. If something comparable is happening with fairies, there should be signs. And if you can find out where and when a huge fairy gathering will occur, you can stave off the Rite."

"Yes, but only at the last possible second."

"Grant, you aren't going to find the kidnapper, no matter how hard you look. From what you've said, preparations for the Rite will leave more traces. Do fairies have any way to learn when and where something like this will happen?"

Grant paused and thought. "I don't know. But I might. Wantest thou to pay a visit with me?"

CHAPTER 15

As THEY were driving to wherever they were going, Forest asked, "So the T-word is why you, Tren, and JX freaked out that morning in the coffee shop, when the girls came in dressed as fairies. For you, that must be a reminder of how little humans know about fairies. Are there other things that I should know that trigger fairies?"

Grant thought for a bit. "It does not bother me much, but many younger fairies cannot stand the fairy cult in fiction. They hate seeing one more story in which being a fairy is a way of writing about coming out: 'I led a hidden life, but now that I had become a fairy, I knew my true self.' Drives them over the edge. Being a fairy is hard and complicated, and they don't like humans using fairies just as a way to talk about something else."

He continued, "JX loves to say, 'I'm waiting to see a fairy story that deals with what it's really like to be a fairy: getting caught in a hailstorm while you are sailing; watching your sails get all chafed and sticky in summer humidity; dating humans and having to walk everywhere; being mistaken for a UFO, of all things. When someone writes that story, let me know. I'll be first in line.'"

Forest thought about what Grant said. It was true that he had associated fairies with little girls in sparkly dresses and overeager souls at the Renaissance Faire. Humans had no clue what fairies were like, even though they lived around them every day, at least in Pine Rapids. To be fair, fairies seemed fairly (fairily?) clueless about people as well.

As Grant drove, they passed through the boxy streets of Pine Rapids. The town had had beautiful Art Moderne buildings built in the first half of the twentieth century, but an urban planner (probably straight) had knocked them down and replaced them with brutalist boxes. The downtown was so devoid of interest that even fans of brutalism were eager to see it knocked down. Forest's gym was one of the few architecturally distinguished buildings, with its golden brick façade and deco trim. Forest loved his gym, and the thought of giving it up because of Grayson's continued to gnaw at him.

After a short drive through many of the uninspiring streets of Pine Rapids, Forest and Grant stopped in a large parking lot in front of two stores, both of which had died during the pandemic. The buildings looked sad, and the city planned to bulldoze them to make room for affordable housing (slums, according to Ray the Compassionate). Forest would have been puzzled—why had they come here?—if time with Grant had not taught him to be ready for anything. The lot had a few scattered cars, most of which looked as if their catalytic converters were long gone. An improbable seagull strutted here and there, even though Pine Rapids was so far from any sea that crabs and lobsters looked like extraterrestrials on restaurant menus. Harsh winters and long neglect had rendered the parking lot a field of potholes, like Mars with less sand.

"Is something going to meet us here?" Forest asked as he got out of the car.

"WATCH OUT!" Grant screamed and pulled Forest to the ground behind a foul-smelling dumpster. A spray of what looked like hail flew over them.

"What…? Get me outta here!" screamed Forest, showing his usual butch side.

"I will, but thou'lt have to move fast. We've been ambushed."

"Ambushed? Who would ambush me?"

"It's not thou, it's me. They're shooting glass shards."

OMG, Grant was right. As Forest had learned, glass shards could kill fairies when not much else could. Panic-stricken, Forest gazed around the parking lot. Everything was moving so quickly that he could not be sure, but he thought he saw figures in green robes. Whether they were sailing or on the ground, he could not tell. His heart was pounding, and he felt the adrenaline pump of sheer terror. What had he gotten himself into?

Grant looked around as well, and after a second, came to a decision. "I need thee to do exactly what I tell thee, no matter how odd it may seem."

"Do I get any advance warning?"

"RUN!" (was the advance warning).

Grabbing Forest's hand, Grant sprinted toward the opposite corner of the parking lot. It was flooded with icy water, which must be why the gulls were there. Sprays of glass shards filled the air.

"Jump!" screamed Grant as he bounded into the middle of the water and disappeared into the depths. Forest paused to overthink at hyperspeed. Should he follow? What if he drowned? What if someone saw him? What if what worked for Grant didn't work for him? What if he could not get up? What if the water was cold and felt icky? What if his clothes got wet? But a voice at the back of his head said, *Someone is shooting glass at you: go!* Even as another voice in his head said, *Don't do it*, Forest jumped.

The shock of the water lasted for less than a second. Forest landed not, as he'd expected, at the bottom of a chilly pond, but in a pit of bouncy balls, like the kind that kids play in at restaurants pretending to be amusement parks. As he climbed out, he saw what looked like a quaint log cabin, surrounded by darkness. Even better, it was quiet. Whoever had been shooting was gone. The cabin door was open and there seemed to be light inside, so he quickly went in. Whatever he had been expecting, it was not this. Impossibly, the front room of the cabin was light and airy, even though underground. Pine scent was everywhere, and the room looked as comfy as could be: beautiful paneling, warm fire, big comfortable chairs.

"Grant? Where are you? Won't they follow us down here? Are we safe?"

"WHO WAKES ME?" said a loud, growly voice. Forest's knees buckled.

But then he heard Grant: "A supplicant, O Parking Lot Gnome, seeketh thy help."

Had he really said "gnome"? Weren't fairies enough?

"GO AWAY," bellowed the voice. Its depth and size hurt Forest's ears. But even as it did, it sounded strangely familiar.

"A gang of fairies is about to use bad magic to control all fairies. I desire thy help to stop them."

"GO AWAY."

"If the gang succeeds, the deaths of thousands of fairies will be on thy hands."

"I'LL CRY INTO MY PILLOW EVERRRRY NIGHT. GO AWAY."

"I'm not going away. I need help."

"CALL DIAL-A-SHRRRRINK."

In a second, the gnome appeared in the main room of the cabin. Forest looked at him—and looked a second time, and then a third. He was so transfixed he forgot all about the ambush. It couldn't be. But there it was.

"Isaac?" he said.

"Forrrrest?" said Isaac.

They were both speechless. Grant looked from Forest to Isaac and back, completely puzzled.

An awkward pause followed. Forest stammered, "I thought you lived with your Aunt Flo in Northeast?"

"I do, but I also live herrrre." Forest would have known that growl anywhere. He heard it dozens of times during the day at his gym. But that Isaac was a gnome was more than he could handle.

Not knowing what to say, Forest just started blathering: "I love your cabin! It reminds me of this place in Maine we went to when I was little that had the same pine paneling. My brother and I used to have to climb a narrow set of stairs up to the second floor, where we slept at night. It got so hot up there! Of course; there was no air-conditioning back then and…."

Grant interrupted, "Forest?"

"Yes?"

"How does thou know the Great Parking Lot Gnome?"

"That's not a parking lot gnome. That's Isaac! He works at my gym, and he's amazing. I've known him forever."

"Forest, Grrrrant is right. I'm a gnome, I was born a gnome, I've always been a gnome, and I'm not going thrrrrough a gnome phase. This is who I am. You didn't think that I was able to fix everything at your gym without a little bit of magic, did you? And, yes, you are safe from the ambushers while you are here. My powerrrr prevents them from following you. But as soon as you resurface, you're on your own."

"But you don't look like a gnome."

"Just watch." In a flash, Isaac shrank into a fat, bearded man, who looked for all the world like a garden ornament. Forest stared and then said, "I see why you prefer a different form." Not his most tactful statement, but truth.

Forest had learned enough from Grant not to trust Disney as a guide to how supernatural creatures looked. But Isaac? Forest was torn: angry at himself for having been so clueless about Isaac, puzzled as to how to help Grant, and unsure what to do or say.

Very awkward pause. Miscellaneous grrrrowls from Isaac/gnome.

Forest took a breath and steadied himself. Grant needed his help to stop the bad fairies. Even though Ray was Mr. Conflict Resolution, Forest was the one who had to resolve conflict at his gym every day—fights over equipment, pay, hours, everything. Anything that people could fight about, they fought about. And Forest had not spent all these years in the fitness business without learning how to handle conflicts.

With a big, bright smile, he turned to Isaac and said, "Isaac, if there's anything I've learned as gym manager, it's that bad stuff that happens in one place affects what happens in another place. If fitness instructors are having a problem, it spills over into the front desk, membership, sanitation, childcare, and so on. If bad fairies end up winning—and right now, chances are looking good—they're going to have imitators. I know zero about gnomes, but if there's any way gnomes could copy the same power play as the bad fairies, they'll try, especially if the fairies succeed. You may think that this has nothing to do with you, and, right now, it doesn't. But it could, and soon."

Isaac looked as if he were about to respond but held back, as if he were thinking over something. Moments passed with some quiet grrrrs. Just maybe, something that Forest said had made sense to him. Or even if Forest was wrong, there was nevertheless a seed of truth in what he had said that made Isaac reconsider. Forest sensed the atmosphere becoming just a little less frosty. Isaac turned to Grant, who had been looking intently at Forest: "So what do you need?"

"News of any new building in Pine Rapids. In the past year or so, dost thou know, or do any gnomes know, of any buildings or parts of buildings that have been remodeled? I don't mean homes. I mean large public buildings, probably downtown."

"Given what you descrrrribe, I can think of two places: the parking lot of the ELH Tower, which just had a total overhaul, and the 7th floor of the Paramount Building, which, from what I've been told, was recently rrrrenovated."

"And that's what I needed," said Grant. "Do you know anything about who was behind the Paramount renovation?"

"They call themselves the Quyrrrre."

"Spelled with a 'qu'?"

"Exactly."

Grant turned to Forest and muttered, "That's exactly what the group hundreds of years ago called themselves when they did the same thing."

"Some people have no creativity. Are you sure they're gay?" responded Forest.

Turning back to the gnome, Grant asked, "What can I offer thee in return for thy information?"

"Five free voyages, wheneverrrr I want."

Forest assumed that Grant would be buying plane tickets for Isaac, but then the truth hit him. Isaac wanted Grant to sail him places. Since Forest had never lived with someone who could sail like fairies, it had never occurred to him that anyone might envy Grant's ability or take advantage of it. But he found himself proud of Grant. Other supernatural beings thought that his sailing was so desirable that it counted as money! He remembered his terrified response to Grant's flying on their first (and so far, only) joint flight together. But if other beings were into it, more power to them. Except…. Should he be jealous? Was it okay for his boyfriend to fly other men? What if they fell? Who would be responsible? A deep well of overthinking yawned before Forest.

"They are thine," said Grant to Isaac, interrupting Forest's downward spiral. "And thanks for thy help. Thou wilt not regret it." He turned to go, leaving Forest and Isaac in an awkward moment.

"See you tomorrow?" Forest asked tentatively. What do you say when you find out your favorite employee is a gnome who lives under a parking lot?

"Watch yourself, Forest. Fairies can be trrrricky," said Isaac.

"I believe you. Anything else I should know?" asked Forest.

Isaac came near to him. Nothing about Isaac indicated his status as a gnome, but Forest was learning that appearances did not mean much in the supernatural realm. Isaac whispered to him, "Grrrrant is a good fairy, but he is fighting big evil. The ambush you both faced today is nothing compared to what the Quyre could do. They will stop at nothing. Watch out."

"I will. Thanks. I guess I'll see you tomorrow?" Forest said quietly, though he was desperate for specifics about what Grant's enemies might do. But he knew that Grant would be waiting for him in the awful parking lot, and he should not have to face the ambush alone, if the green robes were still around. Saying goodbye to Isaac, Forest turned to the ball pit. He didn't want to jump through icy water; he didn't want to be shot at; he didn't want to know Isaac was a gnome. But he had made a promise to Grant. He jumped hard into the ball pit.

He sprang up and into the lot, but twisted his ankle as he landed, the same one he had sprained in his flip over the chair only a few weeks ago, though to Forest it felt as if a lifetime had passed between then and now. He limped to Grant's car as fast as he could, but the shooting of the ambush started again in seconds. After turning around to see the limping Forest, Grant rushed to his side and, saying "Hold on tight," picked up Forest and sailed to the car. In the air, Grant's skilled navigation made it difficult for the glass to come near them. Even as Forest did his best to restrain his terror, he scanned the parking lot, looking for the source of the shooting. He thought he saw the robes again, but they moved so quickly that it was hard to see who or what they were.

In a hurry, Grant threw Forest into the car, dashed to the driver's side, and gunned the car as fast as he could. Forest was embarrassed by his ankle sprain. Grant had had to rescue him as if he were not much better than a damsel in distress.

But Grant had a different impression. "Thou wast astonishing!" he gushed once they were in the car, the heat was on, and conversation was possible.

"You mean how worthless I was, spraining my ankle in the middle of a full-on ambush?"

"No, not that. That could happen to anyone. What I mean is that thou knewest just what to say to get the gnome to change his mind. He was not going to do anything to help. But when thou didst talk, I saw him change."

Though Forest was used to brushing off compliments, he needed this one. Even as his ankle was hurting from the sprain, he was glowing from Grant's praise. With Ray, he had forgotten what admiration was, and it meant a lot to be able to hear a compliment again.

Chapter 16

"THAT WAS so exciting! I haven't been so thrilled since I discovered Fairy Original Liquid on my last trip to London!" gushed Garnel as the Quyre returned from their shootout.

The Quyre inhabited a prefab house on the edge of Pine Rapids in a development where all houses were beige and a hosta in the yard was outré. For some, the development was a perpetual torment, like watching HGTV for all eternity, but the Quyre loved it. Fennel liked that all the streets were alphabetized and arranged in a strict grid. For Eelie, the neighborhood was so quiet that no sounds competed with his customary murmur. Garnel stole Pearson Nut Goodies from the local convenience store and, after a brief disappointment when he learned that the nuts were not what he thought they were, snarfed them down when no one was looking. All were satisfied.

The house had an open floor plan, so the kitchen, dining room, and living room were one continuous space. It was supposed to create a light and airy atmosphere but looked like the deserted warehouses on cop shows where climactic shootouts occurred and villains plummeted to their deaths into pools of bubbling ick.

"Exciting, yes: effective, no," answered Fennel. "They escaped."

"Barely," murmured Eelie.

"Listening to that human scream was hysterical: I had no idea male voices could shriek so high," said Garnel. "Physicists wanting to study subatomic particles should get hold of him and have him scream next to fine crystal."

Changing the topic, Fennel said, "I'm worried. The glass guns that the trolls sold me are light and easy to use, but I worry about their effectiveness."

"Easy to use? It took me forever to load the splinter cartridges. I could have cut myself and been a goner," said Garnel.

Eelie noted, "It would need more than a cut to take down a fairy like me."

"Define 'more,'" said Garnel.

"More than you get from loading the gun," said Fennel.

Eelie turned to Fennel and said, "If we could not stop Grant and his human with our guns, how will we prevent them from disrupting the Rite? That's the real concern since it will become invalid if anything stops it."

Fennel said, "To answer this, we need to understand the discourse of interruption. Interruption occurs when an event in progress is suddenly stopped by a speech act, either by the speaker or by someone else, or an event, either by those involved in the event in progress or by others. Typically, the context …"

Garnel interrupted: "Enough. Answer Eelie's question.""

Looking wounded, Fennel said, "I am making sure that we all understand what an interruption is. Without a clear concept, we have no grounds for moving forward. And I'm not lecturing: I'm explaining."

"No more explaining. We need action," said Garnel.

"What do you propose?" asked Fennel.

"We need an army," announced Eelie.

The room went silent.

"An army?" asked Garnel. "A real army? We've always operated on our own … but I do love men in uniform."

"You think we can find a group of fairies who will fight voluntarily to see us, not them, gain unlimited power?" asked Fennel.

"Fairies appreciate strong leaders. And once we have finished the Rite, we can promise them anything in the world. And we might even give it to them," said Eelie.

"And you think that our army will beat whatever Grant and his human may be up to?" asked Garnel.

"Grant is no fool, but he will never be able to gather an army like ours. How would he even recruit them? He has nothing to offer," said Fennel.

Eelie said, "True. I suspect the cards are in our favor, especially if we start now."

"If we're going to recruit, we need to advertise in fairy venues as soon as possible," said Garnel.

"Too obvious," Fennel cut in. "We can't leave clues that we are preparing a takeover."

Eelie said, "Then don't advertise on obvious sites like GobLinkedIn. There are whole sites on the CobWeb that you don't even know about but that can get us what we need."

"I'm skeptical," said Garnel.

"Ditto," said Fennel.

But Eelie meant what he said. He placed ads on the CobWeb in fairy language. Needing to hint at warrior experience without mentioning it explicitly reined in his usual logorrhea. And, if nothing else, the generous starting salary guaranteed that the ad received attention. Inquiries started filling the Quyre's inbox. There were so many that the Quyre agreed they would have to interview. Since Ray was busy taking care of the Product (Craigy), they agreed to invade his offices and hold the interviews there.

A few days after Eelie placed the ad, the line outside of Ray's Conflict Resolution stretched around the block. When Garnel worried about neighbors, Eelie decided that, if anyone questioned what was happening, they would claim to be selling tickets to a big WWE event (The Purge vs. El Demonio). However long the line was, Fennel was determined to finish the interviews in a few hours, so they would move fast.

As they readied for the big day, the Quyre agreed that they would sort interviewees into "no," "maybe," and "yes." Garnel wanted to provide fay-friendly refreshments (chocolate-frosted elfclairs, millefay, and more), but Fennel quashed that: "The interviews will be strictly business."

The trio looked strictly business in Ray's meeting room. They wore their green robes and sat bolt upright, unsmiling, on uncushioned chairs. Glares that they perfected in their meetings with Ray told interviewees as soon as they entered that the Quyre were serious, and the interviewees responded as if facing a firing squad. While Fennel's ad had tiptoed around the military nature of the enterprise, his first question did not: "An army of fairies is planning to attack us. How would you destroy them?"

Some answers in the "automatic no" category:

Slack-jawed silence. (Eelie liked these interviewees because they did nothing to interrupt his monoversations, but Garnel and Fennel insisted on voting no.)

"How about slowly and painfully?" ("Cringe," Garnel noted.)

"Do you mean 'destroy' like in a Grindr profile, or did you have something else in mind?" (Fennel, not understanding, was going to answer when Eelie and Garnel stopped him.)

Bug-eyed stares. (Eelie also liked these interviewees because he assumed that they were staring at him.)

And many more, from the chunky guy who hummed "Run Away" from *Spamalot* to the svelte redhead who fainted and had to be revived while being pushed out the door, much to the consternation of those waiting for interviews.

Although most were "nos," a few "maybes" surfaced:

"Require your enemy to listen to Ethel Merman's disco album on repeat." (Since the Quyre already knew the effects of nonstop Muzak, this seemed promising.)

"Make your enemy work out to a nonstop stream of exercise videos taught by twentysomethings in neon leotards." (This led to a brief but intense debate among the Quyre about which fitness instructor deserved "most obnoxious.")

"Make them eat cauliflower." (As the Quyre knew, fairies hated cauliflower even more than humans, so much so that cauliflower torture had become a flourishing subgenre of fairy BDSM porn. Garnel could remember when the classic *Cauliflower: Raw, Thick, and Cut* had been the runaway audience favorite at a fairy festival for adult movies.)

"Make them spend a week listening to people in exotic resorts selling them a timeshare." (This option mystified the Quyre, but, since it sounded horrific, they decided it must be a smart way to win a battle.)

And some remained uncategorizable, such as the short, frog-faced fellow who recommended endless push-ups to what he called Springsteen's "Born in the US Fay" and would not back down even when Eelie insisted that he had mistaken the song's title.

But the bottom line was that after hours of interviewing, the Quyre still did not have a single clear "yes."

And then Sandor appeared.

His rugged, handsome face sported a thick beard and a mean-looking scar over his left eyebrow. His arms bulged with muscle, as if he had been modeling for one of the classical Greek sculptors. His dark eyes smoldered even when he was doing the most ordinary things. He towered over all three of the Quyre, who gazed up at him, entranced.

Doing his best to maintain some composure, Fennel asked his usual question about attacking the enemy.

Without missing a beat, Sandor answered: "Classic military tactics are best."

"Such as?" asked Fennel.

"Only one produces consistently excellent results: *penetration of the center*."

He paused while the Quyre looked at each other.

"Details?" requested Eelie.

Garnel added, "When I'm trying to visualize complex maneuvers, it's helpful to have a concrete image. Don't hesitate to act out specifics."

Sandor obliged: "You gather your most powerful, relentless forces and locate a gap in enemy lines, some place that is not guarded and where you can gain a quick entry. Then you make your corps attack that weak spot repeatedly. Your soldiers drive into it over and over again, using all the weapons at their command, until the enemy line is broken. Once you have achieved that objective, you can push deep into enemy territory, and, in my experience, you quickly meet with total surrender." The eyes of the Quyre were glued to Sandor's large, expressive hands as he pantomimed the relentless attack.

"Well, how memorable is that?" gasped Garnel.

"Total surrender," repeated Eelie.

"Your quasi-miming was so helpful. Would you mind repeating it with your shirt off so that we might get a better sense of how you would lead an actual battle?" said Fennel.

At this, Sandor stripped his shirt off in a quick, freeing move. As he did so, his sails billowed out in a stunning white-and-black pattern. He treated the Quyre to a short display of his sailing skills, although the low ceiling of Ray's office prevented him from demonstrating his most breathtaking dives and plunges. It was hard for the Quyre to know where to focus: Sandor's legs, which bulged with his strong quads and hamstrings; his muscular arms and elegant, tapering fingers; or his torso, glowing emerald, with an invitingly hairy chest. The Quyre watched in silent admiration, though an occasional gasp or quiet "Bravo" made their appreciation clear. Sandor was an ideal soldier.

"He's the complete package," said Eelie, after the Quyre asked Sandor to step outside for a minute while they conferred.

"How closely did you look at his package?" asked Garnel.

"No one else even comes close," said Fennel.

"Would I come off as too desperate if I asked him to remove his pants as well as his shirt?" asked Garnel.

"Yes," said Eelie and Fennel, simultaneously. Garnel sulked.

"He has the job. Let's ask him back and let him know," said Fennel.

They did so, and Sandor looked delighted. He asked, "When can I begin recruiting fairies for the army?"

"Immediately," said all three members of the Quyre at once. Fennel continued, "And you should begin with all the fairies still lined up outside. From what we've seen this morning, there's a wide range of experience out there, but they all want to fight for us. Even if they can't lead the army, they may have the makings of good soldiers."

"Leave training to me," said Sandor. "I have a location and equipment that can turn the daintiest fairy into a tough warrior. But I need your help with an incentive, which usually means money."

"I think we can do better than that," answered Eelie.

"You can?" asked Sandor.

"When we have finished what we set out to do, we will be able to make some impressive promises come true," answered Fennel.

"And how will that help me recruit fairies?"

"Tell them that if they fight on our side, a certain part of their anatomy otherwise immune to fairy magic will grow at least one inch longer and several times thicker."

"Seriously? You think that that will be an effective recruiting strategy? I'm not sure," said Sandor.

Fennel and the other members of the Quyre did not answer. They sat and smiled.

Within thirty minutes, Sandor had accumulated the most impressive fairy army ever seen in Pine Rapids.

CHAPTER 17

THE MESSAGE on the phone said, "I need to have a meeting at thy place. My house is being watched." Was the meeting a problem or not? Could Forest get himself in trouble if he ended up doing something that he did not want to do just because he was grateful to Grant? But why did anyone ever do anything, if not for some response from other people? At least so far, he wanted to help the fairies. If fairies helped humans, then having that help taken away or even just limited would be sad. Life, hard as it was, might be so much harder without fairy leveling up.

Happy that his sprain was healing, Forest had been looking forward to a quiet evening after his day at the gym. The response to his water classes had been so enthusiastic that fairies wanted them every day, which meant he had to keep early hours to arrive in time. After a full day of work, he was not up to much. But if Grant and other fairies showed up, whatever his reservations, he could at least let them sit and talk while he spaced out.

Within minutes Grant arrived, along with Tren and JX. Forest remembered seeing them that morning, having a raucous time in the pool. But now faces were grim and brows were furrowed. The fairies were facing an existential threat but were not sure what they needed to do. The attack in the parking lot meant that the Quyre was on to Grant and knew that he was leading the opposition to them. And Isaac's information had let them know where the Rite was likely to occur. But they still did not know when it would happen and, if it did, how they could prevent it effectively.

But that did not stop JX, who offered his plan: "Plant a spy in the Paramount. As soon as he sees the Rite start, we go all Uma in *Kill Bill 2*."

Tren smirked. Forest's eyes grew wide. This was way more butch than he had expected.

Grant interrupted, "If we have spies, they have spies. They'll know what's happening before we even commence. Since the Rite can't be interrupted, they'll have to block access to the rooms. And whatever happens, the child must be safe."

"Well, then, Miss G, what exactly do we do?" asked JX. "When the Fairy Divas are finished with the Rite, you'll be lucky if you can roll over on your perfect sixpack, let alone sail. We have to do something now."

Tren was saying something in response, but Forest wanted to support Grant, who was looking impatient. Not sure what to say, Forest stumbled ahead: "Um… I know I'm not as informed as you are about the situation. But isn't it true that all you have to do is create some distraction to get attention away from what is going on?"

Tren snapped, "Distraction won't stop them."

Forest said, "Okay. It sounds as if you know a lot more than I do about the Quyre. Tell me everything, since I thought that nobody knew who they were."

Caught off guard, Tren and his manbun deflated a little: "How did you know they were called the Quyre?"

Forest paused for a second and then said, "The Great Parking Lot Gnome told me."

Tren looked stunned and a little hurt. Humbled, he continued, "I've never been privileged enough to meet the Gnome, so color me impressed. I don't know the full plans of the Quyre, but they'll repeat what was done before."

"Yes, but they need a kid. Maybe it would be enough just to grab the kid and leave? Without Craig Wallace, nothing can happen," said Forest.

"Yes, but the Quyre will just start again," said Tren.

Forest was going to say that as long as the Rite existed, fairies would never be 100 percent safe. It was like nuclear weapons. As long as there was the technology, destroying weapons would not guarantee safety. Someone could always start again from scratch.

But Grant, resuming leadership, intervened. "One step at a time. Stopping the Rite is the priority. Dealing with perpetrators comes later. Thanks to Isaac, we know that the Rite will take place on the 7th floor of the Paramount. We don't know exactly when, but given that the child disappeared March 1, it will probably be around March 14."

Silence ensued as they thought through options. As they all knew, just walking onto the seventh floor would not help. The bad fairies would detect them and have troops ready with glass shooters. (Having experienced these in the parking lot, Forest did not want to see them again.) Getting there in advance was out. Instead, they had to be ready to go in the nick of time. Getting into the Paramount was easy, but knowing just when the Rite would begin so that they could disrupt it was the challenge. Fairies, for all their powers, were not invisible, especially to other fairies. And given the importance of the Rite, the bad fairies would be ready for them. Nobody in Forest's apartment knew what to do next.

Forest, figuring that he had nothing to lose, broke the silence. "Again, correct me if I'm wrong, but this Rite hasn't been done in a long time. An extraordinarily long time. Does anybody really know how to do it? Do you know if it will even work? Are there any records of what it was like when it was done before?"

The room was silent. Forest had expected to be swatted down with fairy scorn, but to his surprise, Grant, JX, and Tren just looked at each other with what he could interpret only as embarrassment. Had he said something so stupid that the fairies were speechless? Or had this idea never occurred to them before? Was it that they were so used to seeing things in one way that any question coming from a different direction seemed like a bolt from the blue?

Finally, JX broke the silence: "Archive time! Field trip!"

"Is there a Fairy Library of Congress somewhere?" Forest asked.

Grant answered, "There used to be, but now everything's on FayTube, and if you have the right clearance, you can access it all."

"That sounds great, except for one thing," said Forest. "I don't have FayTube, just my sad Lenovo."

Getting up from the table, JX said, "This will take a sec. But don't worry."

Forest immediately worried.

JX rummaged in Forest's kitchen, grabbed a large cast-iron skillet, and went into the alley-like workroom that was Forest's study. Forest followed and watched as JX took the skillet, whooshed it over his head and, pivoting like a baseball pitcher, swung it directly into Forest's computer screen. Forest heard a loud "pop," fizzling electric sounds, and the shattering of glass. JX then clobbered every square inch of Forest's computer with the skillet, shattering keys, leaving wires exposed, destroying the printer.

Forest tried to let out a howl of protest but found that he was so stunned that he had no voice, and it wasn't as if JX would have paid attention anyway. Grant, seeing Forest turn a pale shade of death, rushed over to hold him while JX continued his reign of terror. "It's okay, it's okay, it's okay, it's okay," Forest heard Grant murmur. He loved being held by Grant, but it was not okay. His computer was being reduced to Muesli in front of his eyes. But JX was not finished. He took off his shirt. Although his physique was nothing next to Grant, his skin had the same almost-green tinge to it. And he opened up his sails, which were impressive—if anything, bigger than Grant's—turned his back to the computer, and began to move the sails rapidly, side to side, up and down, front and back, twisting, turning, interlocking, separating, and more. As he did so, the fragments of what had been Forest's computer began to reassemble themselves, but into something that looked different. It was like a fairy version of 3D printing.

Forest, watching, realized that Grant must have used a similar maneuver in their first encounter, when he was able to type words into chat without using his fingers. Fairies continued to surprise him. For all their presence in movies and television, he realized that he knew nothing about them. They were not at all like what they were supposed to be. How many movie fairies took the time to destroy a computer and rebuild it? But that's what JX was doing.

In time, Forest saw a long, lumpy mirror, surrounded by levers of different sizes. The levers looked like an irregular fringe or even mane surrounding oddly textured glass. It reminded him a little of the strange 3D screen that hovered over the jacuzzi in Grant's house when he wanted to watch FayTube. But that was only a screen. JX had created an entire new contraption. JX's fingers pressed the tiny levers in what must have been a precise motion but looked to Forest like a whir, as if he were playing the marimba. Scattered images appeared on the screen, but they meant nothing.

JX, to Forest's surprise, read this morass as if it were simple. Grant whispered to Forest, "Thou'rt seeing fairy texts that are hundreds of years old. The writing and the language were different then, so only specialists like JX can decipher them."

Forest wondered why, if JX were so good an interpreter of ancient texts, he had not already looked at them. Wouldn't that be the obvious first step? Hadn't they watched enough *Scooby-Doo* episodes to know that Velma always did her research first? But he supposed, getting back at the bad fairies had so dominated the group's thinking that they had forgotten the obvious.

"It says something about digits?" commented JX. "Is there a secret combination?"

"I can't imagine why," said Tren. "Never heard about numeric code, just child sacrifice."

"Not just digits," said JX. "Food. The Rite was what they called a 'sumbel' or a spectacular feast."

"Does the Quyre want a replica of the past? Don't they know how yesterday that makes them look?" asked Forest.

Grant said, "They'll want a feast. And fairies can't make food appear out of thin air. Who in town could prepare edibles like that?" Forest's long experience with DoorDash had familiarized him with Pine Rapids fine dining, but not with anyone who could handle catering on the scale that the fairies described.

Tren trawled fairy social media (FayBook, InstaPixie, Puckster) to check out possibilities. JX asked his foodie friends, fairy and human. Although both men worked steadily, after an hour, they had not found a lead. Forest and Grant watched a *Great British Bake Off* rerun, but Forest found that watching people wrestle with *mille-feuille* was not the gripping viewing experience that it usually was. Impatient with the fairies, Forest took out his phone. When he advertised for jobs at the gym, he put ads in all the usual suspects, from LinkedIn to Craigslist, both of which had been surprisingly good ways to find new instructors. He scrolled to Craigslist, searched under "food / bev / hosp," and skimmed what he saw: restaurants wanting new sous chefs, bartenders, line cooks, etc. But about three-quarters of the way down the page, he noticed a listing for "elite chefs and servers needed for high-profile banquet:"

Experienced chefs and servers for an elite, private function in exclusive location. All ingredients, cookware, place settings, serving platters and utensils, and recipes provided by hosts. Servers able to work quietly and quickly, with minimal supervision and interruption. Discretion essential. Pay generous. Send letters of inquiry and list of relevant work experience to fea@gmail.com.

"Grant, look at this!" Forest squawked and passed Grant his phone. Grant pondered it for a while before forwarding the ad to JX and Tren.

"Discretion essential," quoted JX. "It sounds like Grindr. There are so many married men on it that they need to start a Sunday afternoon golf club."

Tren chimed in with "*Fea*? There's proof."

Even though no one said anything, they all felt just a little ill even though they had wanted to find just such information. The ad brought the Rite much closer, even more than the abduction of Craig Wallace had. The Quyre were putting everything in place. If Grant and his men did not stop it, they knew that no one else would.

"Okay, so what now?" Forest asked.

"We apply for the job," said Grant.

"I think all of you would be fantastic waitstaff," Forest said, trying and failing to be supportive.

Without saying a word, JX, Tren, and Grant formed themselves into a mini-semicircle as they stood, facing Forest, silent. Forest felt as if he were confronting a firing squad. "Um… what's going on?" he asked. The others looked at each other, wondering who should speak first.

Grant started by saying, "Thou shouldst not be frightened."

As soon as he heard that, Forest screamed loudly, ran into the kitchen, hid in his broom closet, and slammed the door.

Tren met him there and knocked on the door. "Listen to us."

"Go away!"

JX said, "None of us can do this job. The Quyre will recognize us and know what's up."

"Your problem. Go away!"

JX and Tren began to try to pry the door of Forest's closet open, but Grant held them back.

"Let's talk this through, Forest," he said. "What exactly art thou afraid of?"

"They're gonna kill me!"

Grant answered, "No, wait. The Quyre are not interested in hurting humans. They need humans to staff their huge banquet."

"Excuse me, I've watched every episode of *The Sopranos* at least twice. I know how bad guys behave."

"What's *The Sopranos*?" asked Grant.

"AAAAHHHH. What planet have you been living on? Actually, don't answer that. I get that the Quyre are not interested in hurting humans. But they want secrecy, and the easiest way to get it is to destroy the evidence. In this case, that would mean me, along with any other humans dumb enough to be caught in this."

Grant responded reassuringly, "Thou forgetest. We'll be there."

"I love you forever and a day, but I do not trust you against the Quyre."

"Remember, thou dost not need to be present during the Rite itself. All thou needst to do is to apply to the job and find out the specifics of day and time."

"I haven't been hired! I have no experience as a server except for a summer delivering pizza when I was sixteen, when my garage reeked of roast garlic."

The fairies pleaded:

"Forest, please."

"We'll protect you."

"We would never ask this unless we needed it."

"You are the right man for the job."

"Please step up."

Forest said the only thing he could think of to shut them up: "I need to think about it." It was not the answer that the fairies wanted, but it was the answer that they were getting.

"And, JX, I need my computer fixed." JX left immediately and loud banging noises once again came from Forest's study.

Tren whispered confidentially, "He'll put it back together better. Internet connection will be five times faster. And immune from spam or viral infection." Forest knew he was supposed to be reassured, but the thought of living with a fairy-fixed computer was not something he had ever had to think about. He began calculating in his head the probable cost of another computer. Would he have to break down and buy a laptop?

Grant held Forest by the shoulders and looked at him pleadingly. It took all Forest's willpower not to melt into a puddle and give in. But he had said that he wanted to think, and that was what he was going to do. No more words were spoken. In a few minutes, JX returned, this time with the cleaned cast-iron pan. The fairies, recognizing that talking more would do more harm than good, quietly left. Forest was alone in his apartment, with unsettling thoughts about his future. And they were about to get much worse.

CHAPTER 18

A WEEK had passed, and Ray's condo/sanctuary was unrecognizable. A mural of crayon and Magic Marker had sprung up along one wall of his living room. It reached from the floor to about three feet high and was a maze of color and random patterns, indifferent to the gleaming white latex of Ray's interior paint. Walls not lucky enough to be covered with crayon and Magic Marker were pockmarked with gouges, where they had been beaten with a metal dustpan. Why had they been beaten? Because beating walls with a metal dustpan is fun when you are three and a half years old.

The sharp, surgical lines of Ray's white furniture were gone. Couch pillows, which had always rested just where he would not see them, had been flung everywhere and had gained a tendency to move, as if by themselves, to wherever was most inconvenient for Ray. Ottomans were overturned, curtains pulled down to the floor, Venetian blinds left in gnarls, art glass shattered. Surfaces were blanketed in Cheerios, gummy worms, lollipops, Bugles, chocolate milk, cookie crumbs, and popcorn kernels, popped and unpopped.

Ray's kitchen, hitherto a monument to sterility, had a new veneer. Bits of what might be food stuck to every surface that could be reached, and many that could not. Just how a large brownish blob adhered to a remote corner of the ceiling as it darkened, day after day, to black, was a mystery that Ray would never solve. Juice boxes, which, to Ray's knowledge, had never appeared in the entire condo, let alone in his kitchen, were everywhere. And "everywhere" did not mean "everywhere on the kitchen counter." It meant everywhere—floors, drawers, cabinets, spice racks, utensil containers, the stove surface, the interior of the oven…. Ray had become an expert at making Kraft Macaroni 'n Cheese. He had also become good at eating it since it turned out to be appropriate for breakfast, lunch, and dinner. Not only was he good at eating it, he now could make it in his sleep, as he had proved during a 2:30 a.m. episode when it was demanded, repeatedly, in a tone that would not be denied.

Over Ray's once spotless bathroom, it is best to draw a restraining curtain of charity. Too close an inspection might be so scarring for both reader and author as to require multiple therapy sessions. As for Ray himself, he dreamed of commanding vast armies of bathroom cleaners like the little soap bubbles with faces on commercials, whose help he would summon every fifteen minutes. And morning after morning, he awoke to realize that he had no such armies and that the cleanup would fall entirely and exclusively on him. He did his best, but the odds were against him.

Getting up for Ray used to mean emerging from the pile of satin sheets and beautifully embroidered blankets on his no-longer-unscratched hardwood bedroom floor. But he had given up on his treasured *St*earns and Foster mattress and beautifully inlaid wooden headboard over which he had taken such pains. He had learned, alas too late, that rubber sheets make excellent bedding for toddlers. The bedroom, like the bathroom, was perfumed with the scent of Concentrated Germicidal Clorox Bleach (for Institutional Use Only), which he applied early and often. Although the bleach did not obliterate offending odors, it did overlay them with an equally unpleasant chemical smell. And yet, for all the bedroom's shortcomings, Ray slept there, night after night, exhausted after toddler care.

And there on the bed lay the child. Ray had learned from the media publicity surrounding the toddler's disappearance that his name was Craig, and that "Keggy" was the boy's pronunciation of "Craigy." (He had gotten insulted when Ray, trying to be nice, had called him "Keggy.") Ray had initially dumped a few blankets in the living room and expected Craigy to sleep there. Persistent, ear-splitting howls put an end to that. Craigy made it clear that he was sleeping in the same room as Ray. After Ray carried blankets to his bedroom and put them on the floor, Craigy ignored them and climbed into bed with Ray. Ray, unconscious of Craigy's approach, awoke, finding himself pushed to the edge of the bed while being simultaneously pummeled and kicked by Craigy, deep in the grip of some dream or nightmare. Ray yelled and, as usual, Craigy yelled more loudly. He yelled when Ray picked him up and put him back down on the blankets. He shrieked when Ray put him back in the bed. Evidently, Craigy could sleep only if Ray deserted the bed entirely. Ray knew exactly what people would think if they found out that he had kidnapped a toddler and was sleeping in the same bed with him, but the reality was not at all what people would imagine.

But Craigy's yelling was nothing compared to the drama surrounding "the blankey." Evidently, this object was a sine qua non for Craigy's beauty rest. Ray did not have one. He imagined that the actual object must be disgusting beyond description, so he was not sorry not to have it. But, oh, did Craigy scream. Ray, usually phlegmatic as to push the boundaries of the creepy, at last lost his temper and screamed, "IT'S NOT HERE," in a voice that showed he no longer cared what the neighbors thought. But that was not good enough. In the absence of the blankey, he needed a substitute. As it turned out, his $4,000 Burdeo vicuna sweater (guaranteed product of government-controlled shearing operations), with its graceful V-neck and oh-so-lightweight softness, was (1) soon reduced to a grimy heap of threads and (2) perfect for Craigy— and Ray thought that he had never spent a better $4,000 in his life.

But nothing about Craigy—not his penchant for destroying everything in sight, for launching food into the stratosphere, for urinating on anything that was not moving, for throwing unexpected tantrums multiple times a day—was as challenging as his simple, persistent demand: "Story!" Ray had no storybooks in his condo. He hardly had any books at all, since nobody cool reads books anymore. But Craigy wanted—indeed, demanded—stories.

Ray protested that he did not know stories. Craigy, unmoved, persisted. As Ray soon figured out, his annoyance at Craigy's request made Craigy all the more eager to ask. For Craigy, "Driving Ray up the Wall" was a 100 percent guaranteed ripe Rotten Tomatoes. All hours of day and night, Ray was tormented by "Story, story, story, story, story." But Ray's powers of narrative invention were nonexistent.

Sighing, he did his best: "There was this guy."

Craigy looked, waiting for more.

"And he died. The end."

Craigy had never heard a story like that. Young as he was, he knew something was not right. "Mo," he said. "Mo." There was an awkward pause until Ray realized that Craigy meant "more."

So Ray tried again. "There was this guy. He ate and slept and drank and had a job and lived in an apartment and then died."

Craigy thought about this for a second and then burst out laughing. This was by far the funniest story he had ever heard. "Again!" he demanded. Ray found himself a prisoner of his success. He had a hit, and now his audience wanted it again and again. He tried varying it ("the guy liked pizza" or "the guy made a lot of money") but each variation produced an accusation from Craigy: "Not story!" Irritating as Ray found telling his story over and over to Craigy, he had to admit that this was the first time in his life that anyone thought he had a sense of humor. His clients had always told him, "Ray, we love coming to you because you take us so seriously." Forest had accused him of being a killjoy. He just thought that was because there was nothing amusing about Forest. And as he looked back over his life, he could not remember anyone—parents, siblings, lovers, friends—ever finding him funny.

Until Craigy. For Craigy, Ray was a laugh riot. Part of destroying Ray's condo was just Craigy being Craigy. He had enough energy to fuel Pine Rapids several times over. Yet as Ray came to understand, Craigy destroyed his condo because seeing Ray react was fun. It caught Ray off guard both how ridiculous this was and how much he cared that someone, even just Craigy, was interested to see how he might react to anything. Craigy's "WWWWAYYYYY!" when he was upset, hungry, had hurt himself, or had gotten overstimulated meant that Ray was needed. And being needed was terrifying. Ray had spent most of his life needed by nobody and needing nobody in return. And unexpectedly, that had changed.

Hair-raising as living with Craigy was, it was nothing compared to occasional, unannounced visits from the Quyre. Fennel, Garnel, and Eelie would materialize unexpectedly and gaze at Craigy.

"Delicious," said Fennel.

"So perfect," said Garnel.

"Worth all the trouble," said Eelie.

They apologized to Ray for the inconvenience that he was going through. But they also stressed how what he had done for them in capturing and watching over Craigy would help them in ways that he could not imagine. Even though it might be hard for Ray to believe, they had suffered, suffered terribly. And they were only trying to gain back some of what they had lost or were worried might be lost. At times, Ray could almost feel sympathy for them. While he had no way to know if they told the truth, the sense of hurt and injustice that they projected was genuine. His sympathy was increased by their leaving behind substantial amounts of money each time they visited.

Until…. Garnel let slip a detail of which Ray had been unaware during one of the visits that was closer to the time of the Rite. Fennel and Eelie were conferring, evidently planning some complicated bit of ritual choreography. Garnel, not the brains of the operation, said with a sigh, "Humans can't understand just what the taste means to us. Of course, you all have cravings for whatever—pizza, a martini, a candy bar, ice cream. But those can be satisfied. And none of those is especially good for you. But if you're a fairy, the power that comes from nibbling even just a little bit of human toes is beyond imagining."

"Excuse me. Did you say 'toes' or 'toast'?"

"Why, toes, of course. That's the climax of the Rite. Why do you think we asked you to bother with the Product anyway?"

Ray knew from the apps that some guys were into feet. He always gave them a wide berth. But actually eating toes? This he had never heard and, having heard it, wished he had not. First, it was icky. Second, it would destroy Craigy. Third, much as he, too, wanted to destroy Craigy, something within him knew that the Rite was wrong. Fourth, Ray surprised himself by feeling more strongly about this than he usually did. He did not know how, and he knew how powerful the Quyre was, but as soon as Garnel spoke, he swore to himself that the Quyre would not get so much as a hair of Craigy, let alone his toes. The Quyre may have forced him into abducting Craigy. But they would not force him into letting them hurt Craigy.

What Ray did not know was how to stop them. In this, if nothing else, he was like Grant and his fairies, though he knew nothing of them. He could return Craigy to school or even send him to a police station. He knew that Craigy would be taken care of. But he had seen what the Quyre could do if he got rid of Craigy. Their revenge would be quick and devastating (endless cold and Muzak). And they would only start again with some other kid and some other poor guy suckered into their scheme.

He had one advantage. Since the Quyre were not allowed to touch Craigy until the Rite, they needed Ray to bring Craigy to the Rite itself. He would know exactly when and where it would take place. Based on conversations going back all the way to his first contact with them, he knew that the Rite was on the 7th floor of the Paramount Building, which, as Eelie had explained often, had been renovated just for them.

When he asked the Quyre when he was to bring Craigy, he had always been put off with a "You'll know when you know."

Fennel and Eelie were still eyeing Craigy with what Ray recognized as a hungry leer. Craigy was bowling again with Ray's premium wine collection and was barefoot. Ray saw how closely the Quyre looked at how fast he ran and how healthy his feet looked.

Fennel said, "You've done a better job with the Product than we expected. Given your previous behavior, I expected that you would just lock it in a closet until the Rite. You might consider parenting, even though nothing in your previous history suggests that you'd be any good at it. I'd be happy to spend a few hours with you explaining all you need to know. I know you'll find what I say useful."

"How do I know when you'll need Craigy… um…. the Product?"

Eelie reluctantly turned away from eye-feasting on Craigy and said with imperiousness, "Watch your phone. You'll get twenty-four hours' notice."

So, Ray would have one full day to save Craigy. He had no idea how he would do it, but this conflict was going to be resolved in one way only. The Quyre was not going to get Craigy.

CHAPTER 19

FOREST STARED at his computer screen.

Grant and his fairy buddies had made a strong case for why he had to be at the Rite. But did he really have to apply for a job with the Quyre? They sounded awful. And what if they rejected him? Was he up to the humiliation of being rejected by a bunch of thugs? For a waiter job? How could he even apply for it? He had no experience as waitstaff. His work at the gym gave him a good sense of customer service, but the practicalities of serving food were lost on him except for Mothra. He was a decent cook, though still one who was not ashamed to use Grubhub and DoorDash.

The ad asked for "letters of inquiry and list of relevant work experience." What did that even mean? What did you put in such a letter? Forest thought of openings:

"To Whom It May Concern: My friends want to shoot you full of glass splinters and need me to get information, so would it be okay if I served hors-d'oeuvres at your party?"

"Hear you're planning a blood sacrifice, and I have so many thoughts."

"Having served drinks at numerous massacres, I am ideally qualified for this job. I would include references, but the massacre part makes them hard to come by."

Forest sighed. He would do it for Grant. He would do it for the fairies. He would do it because to not do it was wrong. But he would much rather have been flopped on his sofa watching TV with Mothra.

After numerous revisions, he came to this:

I saw your ad for experienced chefs and servers for your event. As the owner of a gym, Forest's Pool and Fitness, I have many years of customer service experience to help me to do a good job. I learn quickly and can adapt to circumstances. Many years of teaching fitness classes have given me a strong sense of balance, so I believe that I would be good at carrying food and beverages. I have a good eye for arrangement, so if you are looking for someone to help display the food on the table in a way that looks most inviting, I am happy to help. I noticed that you did not provide the date and time of your event. My schedule is open, and I can accommodate almost any time. Thanks for your attention to my letter, and I look forward to hearing from you.

He added on his usual job CV, even though he had zero experience doing anything that the job required. Lying about nonexistent experience was certainly an option, but it was part of Forest's lack of guile that the possibility never occurred to him.

Forest knew that his letter was a snow job and wondered if it might be a good idea to get another perspective before sending it. Ray had been hopeless at such requests: "Why are you giving this to me?" But at the gym, he asked other people to look at any correspondence that mattered, and, oh, had they caught some appalling howlers. For this, he would usually have consulted Grant and his friends, but they were out, and he needed to get this off his desk.

A green icon had appeared on the toolbar at the bottom of his computer after JX had reassembled what he had shattered. When Forest asked about it, Tren told him that it was the fairy version of ChatGPT, called Fair-E. Forest had played around with ChatGPT to help him with advertising language for the gym, so he was used to filling out the prompt box and getting something back from the computer in a few seconds. Curious to see how the fairies would manage gen AI, he clicked on the green icon.

In seconds, his screen erupted and dozens of fairy wings poured into his study, all whirring and twirling on their own, to the accompaniment of the wistful sounds of Barbra Spritesand, one of the fairies' top divas, singing "The Way We Sailed." With the prompt "Comment on the following letter of inquiry, for a job as waitstaff," he filled in Fair-E's search box and pressed enter.

In seconds, a bare-chested redhead with the telltale sort of green torso appeared not on the screen but in Forest's room.

"Who are you, and what are you doing in my study?" asked Forest.

The redhead then produced an avalanche of incomprehensible syllables that Forest realized, after a second, were Fay, the fairy language that Grant and his friends sometimes used, though rarely when Forest was around. After a panicked search on his computer screen, Forest located a tiny "translate" button, which he pressed about six times.

The redhead started again, this time in English. "I'm Fairleigh, the avatar of Fair-E," he said in a mechanical voice. "Who are you?"

Forest gave his name.

"Forest, I have three comments. First, I've read your letter of inquiry. Second, I have some feedback. Third, I want to know if you are ready for it?"

"That depends on the feedback," said Forest.

"I have three comments. My first comment is about sex. Change up positions when you are with another man. Otherwise, it just gets boring. My second comments is about sautéing. Especially with meat, consider mixing olive oil and butter so that you can get the high temperature of the oil plus the flavor of the butter. My third comment is that your letter does not say anything about serving food to people."

Forest took a second to take in this helpful, if unexpected, advice. "Do I get to answer back?"

Dead silence. Fairleigh stared at him blankly. Forest enjoyed staring at Fairleigh's chest but figured he'd better do something to move the conversation. He asked, "Can you give me more detail?"

More silence. This was turning out to be harder than Forest expected. Then he had an idea.

"Hey, Fairleigh, can I answer you back?"

Having heard his name, Fairleigh sprang to artificial life. "I have three comments. My first comment is yes, you can. My second comment is to buy low and sell high. My third comment is that the first hydrogen bomb was tested at the Enewetak atoll in 1952."

Who had taught Fairleigh about what counted as a comment? Intrigued by Fairleigh's answers and wanting an excuse to procrastinate, Forest kept going. "Got it. I want more suggestions about how to improve my letter."

Back to silence. Forest caught himself.

"Hey, Fairleigh, please provide suggestions about how to improve my letter."

"I have three suggestions. My first comment is that you use your customer service experience at the gym to talk about how you relate to people. My second comment is that you talk about serving food. My third comment is that you talk about your experience with cooking."

"Any other ideas? Do you ever have four comments?"

More dead silence. Again, Forest caught himself, and repeated his requests after naming Fairleigh, who responded, "What is four?"

That told Forest what he needed to know. "Fairleigh, thank you for your help."

"Of course. Wishing you a fairy good day."

Ridiculous as Fairleigh was, his suggestions were not bad ones. Tempted as he was to ask Fairleigh to make the changes himself, Forest held himself back. Good or bad, the letter should be his, not anyone else's. Plus, he realized that more time with Fairleigh would mean more sets of three suggestions. Forest suspected that, faced with too many sets of such suggestions, he might take the cast-iron skillet to the computer himself.

At any rate, the "letter of inquiry" was off, as well as his CV. Given his complete lack of experience, the likelihood of rejection or ghostly silence was high. Forest and his boys would just have to get information about the Rite some other way. They were fairies, weren't they? What was the point of being supernatural if you couldn't figure out the plans of your enemies?

After another grueling but rewarding day at work, Forest came home to find a new email on his computer:

"This is the Quyre. We will interview you in thirty minutes. Here is the Zoom link." It was signed "Fennel."

It had never occurred to Forest that he would need an interview. He was expecting a simple yes or no. But ready or not, the Quyre would be on screen in minutes. Forest was tired and ravenous after work. Talking to evil fairies was not how he was imagining spending his evening. Sighing, he went to the kitchen to find what he could bolt down quickly (cottage cheese, coleslaw, and thank heavens for that leftover piece of pepperoni pizza).

What kind of a name was "Fennel?" Grant at least had an ordinary name. JX and Tren had slightly less familiar names, but not as weird as "Fennel," which Forest knew mostly as a vegetable impossible to store because its long, leafy fronds took over the refrigerator, shed everywhere, and had to be cleaned up for the next week. Even if Forest had not known that Fennel was part of a plot to bring tyranny to fairies, Forest would have disliked him just because of his name.

Trying to be presentable, Forest changed out of his usual gym clothes into something more appropriate. He ended up wearing the same shirt he had worn for his first date with Grant because his selection of formal clothes was tiny. The big challenge: pants. Since the meeting was on Zoom, should he risk wearing sweatpants? Should he risk wearing nothing? Tempting though that was, he decided it would be smarter to wear some decent pants just in case he found himself having to get up during the interview.

He set himself up in front of the computer. Consulting for the first time his chair's instruction manual, he learned how to lock it in place so that it would not roll. He tried pushing the chair back, unbalancing it, leaning side to side. It was solid.

Though he was expecting Zoom to take five minutes to update while he joined the meeting, the connection went through smoothly. He saw three faces staring at him: three men in green robes. The one named Fennel was younger but looked deformed; the one named Eelie, middle-aged and somnolent; while Garnel, the oldest, seemed the most out of it.

Fennel began the interview: "We're looking for the absolute best for our engagement. We need experienced and savvy waitstaff for this event who can be ready at short notice. I will now explain the discourse of 'engagement' and provide you with a thorough discussion." Then followed a five-minute mini-lecture in which Fennel explained in detail what everyone already knew. Forest imagined that if Fennel ever got power over all fairies, it would involve not wars or riches but endless lectures, as if fairies were trapped in the most boring undergraduate class ever imagined.

"Short notice is no problem for me," interrupted Forest, lying about his ability to get away from the gym. "I can be there whenever you need me."

"That is important," muttered Eelie, as if interrupted in a one-hundred-year nap.

"We are looking for experienced waitstaff. Your experience was not clear from your letter or CV," said Fennel.

"What is moving in the background?" asked Garnel unexpectedly.

Forest took a quick look around. "Oh, that's my cat Mothra," he said. "She's my pride and joy, and I have lots of experience serving food to her. I always make sure she has several varieties of both wet and dry food."

"So you love her?" asked Fennel.

"More than words can say," answered Forest.

"You'd do a lot for her, I imagine. But let's get back to our ceremony."

Uh-oh, thought Forest. *The killer question. Here goes.* Putting on a big smile, he turned to the camera and said, "I have not had much direct experience serving food at formal occasions, but I enjoy entertaining guests in my apartment." (The first part was true, the second, a lie.) He continued, "As the owner and operator of a gym, I give personalized service to customers. I move quickly among large groups of people and make sure that everyone has the help that they need. I also, as I mentioned, have an eye for design and would help with any support that you might need."

"Hmmmmm," said Fennel.

"Hmmmmm," repeated Eelie….

Garnel would have probably said something but seemed to have nodded off.

"Do you have plans that I might see?" Forest asked.

"I'll share my screen," said Fennel. And soon, Forest saw two displays, marked A and B. A depicted an altar of hewn stones stacked on top of each other, surmounted with an axe and a pile of sticks; B, a silver cage that, from what Forest could tell, had an electrified gate so that anyone who touched it would immediately be zapped.

"Well, these both set a tone, so I'll give you that," said Forest. "But if I may suggest, they are both static. To make a splash at a reception like this, the display needs dynamic elements. A water feature, a track, or a small fire."

He saw Fennel mouth the words "a track" to himself, as if considering the idea. Eelie nodded slowly, as if approving of Forest's idea but about to lapse into catatonia anyway. Garnel, having returned from his trance, nodded enthusiastically. Forest could tell that he had scored a point and hoped that it made up for his inexperience.

Fennel said, "I don't trust you. You do not have the background for this job. But experienced waitstaff with open schedules are turning out to be hard to find. We'll take a risk with you because you seem eager and could use the money, judging from what I can see of your apartment."

Eelie added, "We need more advice. What music do you think would be appropriate for our ceremony?"

That was an easy one. Forest said, "I'm a huge ABBA fan. Their music always puts people in a good mood."

Garnel answered, "What a good idea! We want people in a good mood. It should be a huge party, except for the blood."

"Never heard of them," said Fennel. "I will look into them and see what I think."

"Oh, you'll have so much fun!" said Forest. "*ABBA Gold* changed my life."

"I see," said Eelie.

Fennel ended the interview and directed Forest to keep an eye on his email. The last thing that Fennel said was that he was happy to have met Forest's cat, which Forest would have thought was a strange remark except that everything about the Quyre was so strange that this hardly stood out. And Forest, proud of Mothra as he was, took it as a matter of course that others would notice her as well.

And yet… there was something strange about the way Fennel had made his remark. For a reason that Forest could not pin down, it had sounded less like admiration and more like a threat.

Chapter 20

The next day, exhausted after work, Forest said a quick hello to Charlie on his way up to his apartment, where he was looking forward to Grubhub plus a flop with Mothra. The swimming fairies continued to be his day's highlight, even though it meant getting up early. For some reason, they were big fans of exercise acrostics. He would give them a series of exercises to do, and the first letter of the names of the exercises would spell out a word. This morning, the combo of Frog Tucks / Ankle Reaches / Inverse Jacks / Reclined Kicks / Y Raises ("FAIRY") had gone over big.

But even as he loved teaching the fairies, the bigger picture for his gym was not good. Grayson's was picking off his staff one by one. "Oh, Forest, I'm not going to dump your gym. I'm just going to work at both places." Translation: in time, as schedules shifted and new formats became hot, instructors would dump him. And that was just the start. Clients would flee the second that Grayson's opened. Plans for the grand opening made Mardi Gras parades look tame.

Dragging himself to his apartment, he was so tired that it took him a moment to realize that something was off. Usually, Mothra yelled at him as soon as he entered. It was their ritual. He came in exhausted, and she started a feline *da capo* aria until she was fed, brushed, cuddled, and placated. But Forest knew that small as his apartment was, Mothra had hiding places where she could go if she needed to be alone, so he did not immediately fret her absence.

Until he went to his computer. He saw a heading all in caps, "URGENT."

What now? he thought. The message was from an email that he had not seen before, and his computer told him to guard against emails from out of network. It was probably spam, but he read it just in case:

> *Congratulations! We are delighted to offer you a*
> *position at our event. It will take place on the 7th floor of*
> *the Paramount Building downtown. We will let you know*

the exact time soon. Pay will be $50,000 for around 3 hours of work.

It was such a pleasure to see your cat that we have taken her. She will be treated well as long as you follow directions. We know that you have become close to a fairy named Grant because we saw you both in the parking lot near the gnome's home. Grant is tracking us, and we suspect that he will try to disrupt the Rite. Since you have no experience as waitstaff, you can at least help us by informing on Grant. We expect regular updates from you about what he and his associates are doing. If you tell him about this communication, your cat will be killed. If you tell anyone about this communication, your cat will be killed. We are watching you at all times. Do not try to escape. We will return your cat when we have destroyed Grant and his followers. Cross us at your cat's peril.

The Quyre: Fennel, Eelie, and Garnel

PS: You were right about ABBA. They are the perfect choice. We also like the idea of a track.

"NOOOOOOOOOOOOOOOOOO." A shriek so piercing that it made Fay Wray and Janet Leigh sound like bass baritones. Forest's blood froze. He read the email once in disbelief and then read it again more carefully. Mothra! He didn't believe it and ran through the apartment yelling her name as sweat poured from his body. She was nowhere to be found. As he searched, he cursed himself. Why hadn't he done more to protect her? Why hadn't his apartment been more secure? Why had he not trained her to attack anyone trying to nab her? What was happening to her now? He was sure she was being held in some filthy dungeon, starving and growing matted from neglect. Who would give her water? Who would brush her? Who would do yoga with her? Who would talk with her and sing her theme song?

Even worse, how could he have been so stupid? Of course the Quyre were the figures who had shot at Grant in the parking lot. He had even seen them with his own eyes. Of course they would know he was Grant's boyfriend. The whole interview had been a trap to get him to spy on Grant for them. And now that trap included Mothra, who had done nothing to deserve being kidnapped. How stupid he had been! Ridiculous as the Quyre was, they knew how to set a trap and spring it, and now he was in their power.

Forest's thumper neighbor who was convinced he was a sign of the apocalypse pounded on his door.

"What is going on in there?"

"Mind your own business," Forest screamed, not believing that this was happening. "Go away. I don't have time for you."

"I'll tell Charlie that screams are coming from your apartment."

"Knock yourself out."

Forest's fury at his neighbor reminded him that people lied all the time. How did he know that the Quyre's email was true? Maybe it was all a lie and they just wanted him to think they had Mothra. Before he acted, he needed proof, and proof that she was being treated well. If they wanted something from him, they could answer a few questions.

He wrote back: "Burn in hell, you assholes. Give me my cat back now. Or else."

Email pause.

"Or else what?" came the reply from Fennel.

"Or else I will track you down and destroy you and everyone you ever cared about."

"Aren't you young and sweet and a bit over seventeen? We have Mothra—" (How dare they use her name!) "—and we will give her back, if we give her back, when we are ready." This email was signed "Eelie" and "Garnel," also accompanied by selfies.

Forest hurled himself away from his computer and began pacing. As he did so, he screamed howls of frustration, anger, and fear, the kind that left you hoarse for hours afterward. If Charlie came, who cared? He had never screamed so loudly since a kidney stone took him to the emergency room. He pummeled his sofa, hammered his bed, pounded on the walls, stomped his feet, and cursed. If he had had much in the way of glassware to shatter, he would have shattered it. It had all become too much: his gym, Grant and the fairies, and now Mothra. What had happened to his life?

After a time, he wore himself out and stood stunned in the middle of his living room. His thoughts were racing, and he was having a hard time knowing what to do next. On TV, whenever there was a kidnapping, police always wanted proof that the victim was alive and as safe as could be expected. For the time being, cursing the Quyre would not help. They had power, not him, so he had to find a way to work with them. That would begin by asking for proof that they had Mothra and, more, that she was being treated well. He went back to his computer.

"Let me see her. Prove to me that you have her. If so much as the tiniest hair on her head has been damaged, all deals are off."

Another pause.

After a few minutes that, to Forest, felt as if they took longer than a Pride parade, an email appeared headed "Livestream." It had nothing but a link, which Forest clicked. Another pause that was short in real time but endless to Forest, and a camera feed appeared.

At first it was just a blur.

"Mothra, where are you, my baby? Daddy's here! Where's Mothra? Where's my girl?" Forest yelled, hoping that somehow the camera feed would carry his voice.

With painful slowness, the picture cleared. Mothra was enthroned on a puffy pillow in what looked like a basket made of gold. She was in a familiar meatloaf position, staring straight ahead. The background showed elaborate cat towers and a sea of cat toys, far more than Forest ever had in his apartment.

"Oh my God! What have they done to you, my poor baby! It kills me to see you like this."

As Forest choked, gagged, and sobbed, Mothra looked blankly at nothing in particular.

"I can't bear it! What monster would be capable of such cruelty?"

The camera followed as Mothra sauntered to her feeding dishes, which, again, looked made of gold. Forest could not quite tell what they had been feeding her, but Mothra dug into whatever it was with relish. One elaborately carved dish had what looked like wet food, another had dry food, and a third had water. All were abundantly supplied.

Forest screamed, "Oh my God. They're starving her! She's starving! Nothing but skin and bones! Don't worry, baby! Daddy is coming with lots of yummy food for you."

Mothra licked her right paw, yawned, and ate more.

"What are they doing to you? God, that my sweet cat should be tortured like this! The sick, twisted inhumanity! Oh my baby, do what you need to do to survive, sweetheart. You deserve so much support. As soon as you're home, we'll get you the best veterinary therapist in the world. You're such a big, brave girl."

Mothra went back to her gorgeous bed, walked around it several times, curled up, shook her head, and appeared ready for a nap. Her head nestled near her feet to make a big cat donut. A message appeared on the live feed, "Feed ending in ten seconds," followed by a countdown.

"My girl! I can't bear to see you in agony like this. Be brave. I promise Daddy is coming for you. Just be strong until I get there. I love you, I love you, I love you—"

The feed cut off just then as Mothra fell asleep. Forest burst into hysterical tears.

Forest felt sick. He was ill with worry about Mothra, frightened for Grant, furious with the Quyre, with Grayson, with everyone who was destroying his life. His stomach heaved and he knew he was going to be sick. In a blur, he ran to his bathroom, threw up in spasmodic heaves, and collapsed crying on the floor. There, in his tiny bathroom, on the ugly terrazzo floor, he could see the dingy walls, the toilet in need of a better cleaning, the shower curtain that needed to be replaced. But none of that mattered. All that he cared about was Mothra. He had to get her back.

Forest had never felt so alone. He could tell no one about what was happening. People would just think that he was stressed because he had lost a cat. They had no idea. How could they? Just at the moment when he needed people more than ever, nobody was there, just like "Send in the Clowns." He had tried his whole life to be kind to everybody, and now, at his moment of crisis, he was alone. And that meant, as usual, that no one else was going to get him out of this mess: no police, no detective, no knight in shining armor, no nothing. No one else was going to get Mothra back. No one else would crush the Quyre. It was up to him.

When he at last climbed onto his knees and pushed himself up, the overthinking had been burned out of him. It was time to act.

"I don't know who the Quyre are or what they think they're doing. But they don't know who they're dealing with. I don't care if they're fairies or humans. They are not going to beat me, and they are not going to hurt my cat."

Almost involuntarily, he found his hands curling into fists, as tears continued to stream from his eyes. In his head, he could hear an offstage orchestra swelling, even as his voice came and went between his sobs.

"I'm not going to let the Quyre lick me or anyone I love. I'm stronger than I think I am. You don't become a gay adult man without knowing how to beat your enemies. One rep at a time, that's how I get through this. I don't know how I'm going to do it, but when it's all over, I'll be better and more fitter than ever before. It's the reps you don't want to do that give you the most benefit. I swear I'll never be catless again. Yes, it will be hard work, but the payoff is worth it. If I have to lie, cheat, steal, kill, or do even more reps—as God as my witness—as God as my witness—I'LL NEVER BE CATLESS AGAIN."

At the moment when there should have been a huge orchestral swell with Mothra's theme song, he heard instead a knock on the door.

"Forest, this is Charlie. I'm getting complaints that screams are coming from your apartment."

Forest went to the door and opened it a crack.

"Charlie, it's Mothra. She's… in trouble. I just found out, and the stress is killing me. But I'll quiet the screaming. Sorry to make trouble for you."

He shut the door, fuming. He paced around his apartment, trying to figure out what to do next. What would he do about Grant? Much as he loved Grant, Forest did not want Grant asking about why he had been crying. Grant would be so sweet that Forest would not be able to stop himself from telling him, and then what would happen to Mothra?

After about forty minutes of high stress, he heard a knock that he immediately recognized as Grant's. What would he do?

"Thanks, beautiful. Good to see thee, as always," said Grant as he came in. "I need thy advice. I made a trip to the Paramount today to examine the seventh floor. I'm going to show thee the pictures that I took so that we can brainstorm ideas about how to disrupt anything that may happen there. What do you think of the renovation?"

Forest, obsessed with Mothra, had not heard a word that Grant had said. But when he saw Grant looking at him expectantly, he pretended to brighten up: "Pictures! I always love looking at pictures. I still remember how impressed I was with the ones that you sent of yourself soon after we met."

Grant grinned, though he noted, "Thou soundest a tad hoarse, and thine eyes are red. Art thou okay?" Forest reassured him that it was just allergies (even though it was March and Pine Rapids was still frozen), and Grant, taking out his phone, maneuvered so that Forest could see. He scrolled through the photos of what looked like a ghastly renovation in one of Pine Rapids' few distinguished buildings. Glaring overhead lights competed with too-bright terrazzo and alarming yellow desk accents. It made Forest's head hurt just to look at the pictures. He hoped that Grant would not notice how distracted he was and prayed that he would not notice that Mothra was missing.

As if on cue, Grant asked, "Where's thy cat? She usually comes to the door when I enter to see if I'm going to give her food."

Forest felt his stomach go clammy. "Do you mind if we sit down? I wanted to chat with you about the water exercise classes. Do the other fairies like them?"

"Like them? They're in raptures! As I have recounted, fairies usually do not have freedom in the water, and your class is bringing them joy. I've seen fairies try things that, so far as I know, fairies have never tried before."

"That's nice of you to say."

"Simple truth."

"I have a sequence for tomorrow that I'm really excited about. Can I run it by you? Kicks / Inverse Jacks / Dolphins / Nose to Knee / Ankle Reaches / and Pops. Is it too easy?" He said each move slowly and prayed that Grant would understand. Sometimes Grant could be clueless, and Forest prayed that this would not be one of those times. He gazed deep into Grant's eyes and tried to send him a message of panic.

"Could'st thou repeat that list for me?"

Forest obliged. And there was a pause while Grant considered. They looked at each other. Forest tried to shake his head in an infinitesimally small way to prevent Grant from asking awkward questions. Grant looked pleadingly at Forest. He clearly wanted to know everything, but he would also know that, if Mothra had indeed been kidnapped, the Quyre would be on top of Forest for information.

Suddenly, Grant said, "I think I should go."

Forest turned as white as a character in *Frozen*. But he did not stop Grant from leaving. And he did not remember falling asleep at the table. After all that had happened, he was so tired that he put his head down, and in a minute had passed out with exhaustion.

The next morning, he awoke to the saddest email he had ever received:

"Forest, I love thee, but we need to see less of each other. The situation with the Quyre has eaten up time, and I cannot give thee the attention thou deservest. When it's over, we will see where we are and if we want to move forward. But for now, we should pause. I'll still see thee at the pool."

His head in his hands, Forest felt his heart finally break. His business was dying, his cat was gone, his gorgeous boyfriend had just dumped him. It could not get any worse, except it was bad luck even to think that because as soon as you did, things would get worse. He prayed to himself that Grant was breaking up with him as a move against the Quyre. But was that just wishful thinking? It would be better for Mothra if Grant kept his distance. It would be better for him if Grant kept his distance. But what if Grant found someone else in the meantime? What if he decided that he liked not having to see Forest? And all this for a guy that he had not even had a chance to have sex with, desperate though he was for it. Forest had bottomed for so many drips and here, with a man (well, male fairy) a hundred times over the most beautiful that Forest had ever seen, he had not even gone all the way.

The next morning, Forest began life as unwilling double agent. He saw Grant at the pool, and Grant always flashed him his smile. But that was all. He no longer went to Grant's house, had alone time with Grant, or saw Grant in his apartment. Their relationship had been inadvertently Platonic, despite their best efforts. Now, it was deliberately Platonic as they kept their distance from each other. Forest told himself that it was best for everyone, that it was the smart thing to do, that it was what Grant would want, and felt as gloomy as the audience at the end of *Les Misérables*.

Every few days, he emailed Quyre some information about what Grant, Tren, and JX had already done before Grant had broken up with him. He parceled out the information a sliver at a time. One day, he wrote, "They know about the Rite." Another day, "They expect that there will be lots of food at it." Forest kept his emails short and bare bones. There was no reason to give the Quyre more than was essential to keep Mothra alive.

He suspected that the Quyre already knew most of what he told them: "Grant knows about the child;" "The Rite will give you great power in the fairy world;" "No one has performed the Rite in hundreds of years."

Once, Fennel had even fired off an irritated "Is that all you have to tell us?" in response to one of Forest's particularly bland emails. But Forest kept them coming, following the Quyre's instructions without giving them enough to have an advantage. In return, every few days, the Quyre allowed him a five-minute livestream with Mothra, which left him a blubbering wreck and left Mothra looking as indifferent as always.

But there was more. One day, the following appeared: "In three days, you will attend the Rite. It will commence at noon on the 7th floor of the Paramount. If all goes well, Mothra will return to you then."

Forest's head crowded with questions. He'd have to remember to take the day off from the gym. It was the 9th, so three days meant the 12th. He wondered if Grant already knew about the date and time. If Forest told Grant directly, he would be disobeying the Quyre's instructions and putting Mothra's life in danger. But if he did not tell Grant, then there was no way that Grant and his allies could stop the Rite. The suspense had been bad before and it was worse now. Forest kept telling himself that he had to act and act now, except that he did not know what to do. But he did know this. He would be playing a bigger role in the Rite than he had ever imagined.

CHAPTER 21

March 10, 6:30 p.m.

HOME AFTER work, Forest took out his phone to talk with Grant, realized what he was doing, paused, and put it away. So much he wanted to say—but the less Forest knew about what Grant was doing, the better. The usual "?" email from the Quyre sat in his inbox, waiting for an answer. As always, that answer had to be true, even revealing, but could not hurt Grant. Forest answered with what he considered a masterpiece of concision: "I think they know." He omitted a direct object for the verb so it was up to the Quyre to figure out what "they" knew. The more he worked as a double agent, the more he felt the regress of "they know x because I told them, and I know that they know x, and they know that I know that they know x, and I know that they know…." In the end, the messages did not matter. The Quyre knew that he was in their power, and that was all that mattered to them. Also, both sides knew that, despite information in advance, the Rite was going to be a huge confrontation, like the Battle of the Somme with better hair. Nothing could stop it.

And then came an email from the Quyre that was strange even for them: "The Rite is tomorrow at 4:15 a.m. Bring saffron custard."

Forest went from being tired and cranky after a long day at work to panic mode. The Quyre had changed the time of the Rite! Forest figured that they must be trying to throw off Grant. Forest had a challenge ahead. He had to get this information to Grant without the Quyre finding out. He ran through in his head a thousand scenarios for communicating with Grant, but all had drawbacks that threatened Mothra. The Quyre were everywhere and saw everything.

With one exception.

Forest ran down the flights of steps in his apartment to get to the garage, gave a quick hello to Charlie, got in his car, and flew to the cold and depressing home of the Great Parking Lot Gnome. He and Isaac had never talked about fairy business at work, though he did notice that when no one else was listening, Isaac would sneak up on him and provide a "grrrr." Forest and Isaac continued at Forest's gym as if their parking lot encounter never happened, although there was a newfound respect in Forest's treatment of Isaac. But now Forest was desperate. He had to speak to someone.

The March snows of Pine Rapids were rapidly melting. The pool of water over the entrance to the gnome's dwelling was deeper than ever. Forest took a flying jump, landed in a freezing cold puddle, and discovered that he was soaking wet and cold, but not in the gnome's dwelling. The puddle was so large that it was no longer possible to tell exactly where you had to jump, and Grant was not here to help him. To make the job even harder, the March sun in Pine Rapids set early. Even though it was around 7:00 p.m., the night was dark, and lights in the parking lot illuminated little. Forest waded through the puddle here and there, getting his boots and pants soaking wet and freezing. Over and over again, he jumped only to find that he was splashing cold water everywhere, mostly on himself. If anyone saw him, they would treat him as an adult trapped in childhood fantasies of jumping in puddles. But he was not a child. He was a man who wanted badly to be back in his apartment, with Grant on one side and Mothra on the other. But both were gone.

Forest jumped and jumped and jumped again. He could not look more ridiculous or more helpless. Though it would not help him with his problems, a good scream might at least vent his frustration. He charged forward and treated the gulls in the parking lot to a primal scream the likes of which they had never heard, at the end of which he disappeared, much to the surprise of the gulls. Down he went, once again into the ball pit. Unfortunately, his primal scream during the jump meant that a good quantity of cold, dirty water from the parking lot entered his mouth before he landed, so his entrance was accompanied by near drowning. In the ball pit, he coughed, spit, hacked, and wiped his mouth as if he had just finished a bad blowjob. Thank heavens Grant was not there to see him look so miserable.

But Isaac was. "Forest, stop spitting all overrrr my property?"

"Oh, Isaac." Isaac glared…. "I mean, Oh Great Parking Lot Gnome…." (Hack hack gasp.) "Just give me a minute." (Wheeze.)

"I don't have much choice."

Forest struggled to get his breath.

"The Quyre have changed the date of the Rite"—Gasp.—"to tomorrow at 4:15 a.m. and someone needs to tell Grant." (Cough cough.)

"Grrrr… and who exactly is 'someone'?"

"If I tell him, the Quyre will hurt Mothra."

"Who?"

"You know Mothra. I talk about her all the time at work. The Quyre kidnapped her and promised to hurt her if I told anyone about what they were doing."

"Ouch."

"I came here because you are the only person… being?… supernatural creature?…." Forest was starting to evaporate into a cloud of overthinking.

"Stick with 'perrrrson.'"

"Thanks. The only person who has a shield against the Quyre's ability to see everything. Please help me?"

Long pause.

"How much is it worrrrth to you?"

"Enough that I just re-enacted *Titanic*, jumped into a freezing cold monster puddle, and swallowed way too much disgusting water in the parking lot, just to speak to you."

"I meant, what will you give me in exchange?"

"What do you want? A promotion? A different job? A better office? Let me know."

Isaac smiled. "I want to see you and Grrrrant happy together. That last guy—what was his name?—was a loser. You deserve better."

Kindness caught Forest off guard. He was speechless. Isaac had every right to ask a favor of him, and instead, he had just wished good luck to him and Grant. They needed it. But it moved Forest almost to tears, and through the last stages of his gagging and choking, he whispered, "Thank you."

Returning the whisper, Isaac said, "I'll see that he knows. But rrrremember, the Quyre could be playing you as well. The real time may be something else entirely."

The thought had occurred to Forest, but he had received his instructions and was too frightened to disobey. He would be at the Paramount as requested, at 4:15 a.m. With saffron custard.

On the way home, Forest started on his next major project: making the custard. By 8:30 p.m., he was at the local store buying quantities of eggs, whole milk, cream, and saffron, enough to come close to bankrupting him. His culinary goddess Mina Flowers had no recipe for saffron custard. He had stooped, with a sense of betrayal in his soul, to Martha Stewart, who did have a recipe (he prayed Mina would forgive him). It took many tries. Aiming at a custard, Forest produced, on more than one occasion, college dining hall scrambled eggs. Maybe he could just add McCormick yellow food coloring to store-bought Jell-O pudding. Would the Quyre notice? Finally, at around 1:30 a.m., after a string of failures, the ingredients gelled just enough, and his clunky, antiquated Pyrex dish was filled with a pale-yellow custard. He would love for it to have a beautiful crème brûlée char on top but feared he would burn his apartment to the ground. Enough was enough. Forest packed the custard and waited. The Rite was starting shortly, and he would be there as instructed.

2:00 A.M.: In the pool at Forest's gym, Grant's fairies were restless. Grant was proud of them because ever since the morning of the graunt, they had been doing more than just attending Forest's morning class. They also, deep in the night, met in the pool to practice fairy military maneuvers. Though he encountered the expected amount of fairy silliness, Grant had been impressed with how seriously his fairies took the operation. Tren had somehow managed to reproduce Forest's keys when he was not looking so they could sneak into the pool area, and they had been careful to get out before Forest arrived for the morning class. That way, Forest could let them in without knowing that they had actually been there for hours already. Grant felt a little bad about tricking Forest, but it was all for a good cause. Moreover, as far as Grant could see, the fairies had been scrupulously respectful of the gym. No matter how boisterous the maneuvers had gotten, the pool was always spotless in time for Forest's class.

Grant had found out, through fairy connections, that the Quyre had recruited many followers with their promises (though the exact nature of those promises remained vague). He even knew that Sandor was leading the Quyre's followers, who would be well armed, probably better than Grant's fairies would ever be. But Grant repeated the plan that they had all heard many times:

"When we appear, the Quyre guard will unleash a barrage of glass from their guns. That's why we all have a shield. Parry as much glass as possible. To reduce the likelihood of anyone getting hit, we scatter as soon as we enter and move as fast as possible. This will make it harder for them to hit all of us, because we won't appear as a clump. Also, make sure to vary the height of your sailing, for the same reason."

Grant remembered with embarrassment the first time the shields had appeared. Although all the fairies started pretending to be Captain America as soon as Grant gave them their shields, these were not little round shields but substantial shoulder-to-floor shields that covered most of the body. It was not clear what they were made of, but it looked like solid rock. Yet they were surprisingly light, though dense enough to deflect any glass shards that might come at them. But the fairies had not anticipated that the shields might cause them to bump into other fairies during maneuvers or that the weight of the shields might interfere with their sailing. They all remembered the night when, after watching them practice, Grant told them, "If that's the best you can do, the Quyre has won." After that slap in the face, their navigation skills had improved, Grant was happy to note.

Over the following nights, as they readied themselves for battle, Grant made sure to have them maneuver in every possible direction and formation. Slowly, they began to look more prepared, small in number though they were. Grant and his fairies all knew the stakes in this battle. If the Rite succeeded, they would give up everything they knew and loved. They had to win. Although they all understood how well armed the Quyre would be, victory no longer looked quite so inevitable, despite all the Quyre's money. With a little bit of cleverness, Grant's men might defeat them, even if they did not yet quite realize it.

UNSEEN BY the fairies, Isaac had begun to watch their maneuvers in the night. Although, as the Great Parking Lot Gnome, he was bound to neutrality in this fairy war, he could not help wanting to see what would happen to Grant and his men. Forest's point that the Quyre's success might embolden renegade gnomes to do something similar had hit home with him. In spite of himself, he could not help wanting Grant's fairies to succeed.

2:30 AM: After the usual macaroni and cheese, bath, story, and campaign to dominate Ray's bed, Craigy was asleep. Ray was awake but sat as still as a patient during a colonoscopy. The Quyre had given him specific instructions about just when he was to arrive with the child. For the hundredth time, he imagined not taking Craigy to the Rite, not giving the Quyre what they wanted, not holding up his end of the non-bargain bargain. He envisioned leaving Craigy outside his day care. Everyone would be happy to see him again. Craigy would adapt to his previous life and forget all about Ray, the condo, bad macaroni and cheese, and Ray's silly story. Best outcome ever.

But the Quyre needed their Product. And Ray had promised it to them.

The alarm rang in the middle of the night. With greater gentleness than he had handled anything in his life, Ray scooped Craigy up from bed in what remained of his vicuna. Craigy was deep in sleep. Ray hoped that he might just sleep through the whole thing, though he knew how unlikely that would be. Holding Craigy slumped on his shoulder, Ray left the condo. He felt like Renfield bringing Dracula new prey.

As Ray tiptoed to his car, he kept hoping that something, somehow, would interrupt him and prevent him from delivering Craigy, as always happened in the movies. Nothing did. Traffic was light; the night was cold and clear. Much to his surprise, he found a place to park near the Paramount Building (during the day, he would have had to search for blocks). Craigy murmured, "Where going?" as Ray carried him out of the car.

"Sssshh. Back to sleep." Much to Ray's surprise, Craigy fell back to sleep. After creeping into the Paramount, Ray pressed the elevator button to the seventh floor.

3:30 A.M.: On the seventh floor of the Paramount, Fennel, Eelie, and Garnel faced their followers. There was a faint hum of conversation, which Fennel soon interrupted.

"As you know, forces against us will try to interrupt and destroy the Rite. Your job is to stop them. Let me now explain the discourse of 'stopping.'" Fennel continued for the next twenty minutes to lecture about what "stop" meant. Most of the followers stood at inattention, picking their noses, texting each other, staring at the ceiling, fantasizing about money promised to them when the Rite succeeded. They looked as if they wanted to do almost anything else. Only Sandor, a beefy fairy and head of the Quyre guard, stood solidly at attention. Fennel, oblivious in his monoversation, kept talking.

At last, Eelie interrupted: "We must open the arsenal."

He turned to a large rectangular vault with a complex lock that had dials within dials. The followers waited for him to work the dials, since they had never seen such a complex lock before. As JX had done with Tren's computer, Eelie turned his back to the lock, opened his sails, and went through complex, intricate maneuvers, all the while murmuring softly about how unappreciated he felt. Garnel nodded sympathetically. Fennel's eyes glazed over. Some followers even sat down against the wall and closed their eyes as Eelie droned on.

At last, a deep shudder came from the vault. With a great cracking, the vault opened. It was not clear if Eelie's sails had opened the vault or if he had just bored it into submission, since the vault split exactly in two, with a top half and a bottom half that made it look like a mouth yawning. The followers, having been droned into catatonia, now rushed to seize weapons. They were the same as the ones that the Quyre had used against Grant and Forest in the gnome's parking lot: guns that shot bolts of slivered glass. The challenge with them was friendly fire, especially because the glass flew everywhere. But Sandor had made sure that the Quyre's posse had been practicing in the Paramount for days. They knew how to shoot the splinters and how to avoid them when they were shot at. They checked each part of the guns, loaded them with cartridges of glass splinters, and made sure that the holo sights were working. The holo sights were lighter and easier to handle than the human versions and, in the hands of an experienced user, which they all were, lethal.

The Quyre's preparations had been serious. The Rite would be defended with the full skill of a trained fairy militia. Although they knew the consequences of the Rite, the Quyre had promised them so much wealth and power that they did not mind ceding control to Fennel, Eelie, and Garnel. Many of them had not come from privileged backgrounds, and the prospect of a life with money was enough to make them do almost anything. Being a fairy was all well and good, but poverty sucks no matter whether you are human or supernatural.

Chapter 22

EXACTLY AT 4:15 a.m., Forest knocked at the door of the Great Hall of the 7th floor of the Paramount.

"Hey, dude!" said Grayson, opening the door.

Forest stared. Grayson? With the Quyre? Forest realized that the Quyre was not just about fairies. They were aiming bigger. Grayson's presence meant that they had seduced/coerced humans to take part in the Rite, presumably for a big reward. Forest wondered if their ultimate aim was to dominate both the human and fairy world together.

As the silence between them grew awkward, Forest muttered, "I brought the custard, as requested."

"That's awesome, dude! You can put it with all the others on the table near the back of the room. Wow, those fairies do love their custard. Oh, and while you're here, thanks so much for doing such an awesome job training all your instructors. I know if they've worked for you, they're top of the line, and I can hire them without a second thought. It's such a relief, and I have you to thank."

Forest had nothing to say to this, and so, squeezing past Grayson's steroidal bulk, he entered the hall. It was lit with what seemed to be thousands of candles but were actually jars emitting a weird green glow whose source was not apparent. The Quyre had not deceived him about the time because the room looked ready. Large curtains in front of the windows had been closed to highlight the eerie glow. Human servers had already covered long tables with layers of embroidered cloth to prepare for the feast. Napkins were especially elaborate: luxury mint green pieces of the finest polyester. In addition, Forest saw what looked like Glamour Gourmet single burners glowing red. He heard Grayson explaining that they had been prepared in advance to make sure that the food never fell so much as a degree below optimum temperature.

Most important, tucked away in a corner, he noticed a pet carrier. He flew to it, fell to his knees to open the gate, and yelled, "Mothra!"

But just as he was about to scoop Mothra into his arms, Grayson appeared and shut the gate hard. "Dude, you'll get your cat when the Rite is finished, not before."

If looks could kill, Forest would have annihilated Grayson right there. But the best he could do was to murmur words of love and encouragement to Mothra, who stared at him blankly from the confines of the carrier. "I love you, I love you, I love you. I promise Daddy will be back as soon as he can, and we will get out of here and go home."

"Dude, get a grip. It's just a cat."

Forest wanted to use one of his Krav Maga moves to strangle Grayson, just because it would feel so good to see him squirm. Instead, he walked away fast toward the center of the hall, where he saw Fennel nagging an oppressed young man, who was operating what looked like an elevated Lionel train set but was a conveyor belt on a platform, covered with mock-grass. The empty conveyor belt crawled as if waiting to be adorned with second-rate sushi. Suddenly, he realized that the train track was his fault. He was the one who had recommended "a track" to the Quyre. This was not what he had had in mind, but this is what the Quyre had done with his suggestion.

Fennel raged at the trembling young man that he had had the track imported from Taiwan, custom-made, after numerous Zoom lectures to baffled Taiwanese service people. Prominent on the belt were two goal-post-shaped brackets, about three feet apart, that moved along with the belt and were just big enough to hold a small child. The young man trembled under the table while he supervised the gears turning and made sure the belt tracked on its rollers. Fennel had tasked him with keeping the belt running smoothly and informed him that the consequences of its not running smoothly would involve painful, lasting consequences to his nether regions. Terrified, the man was sweating buckets, as if in the final stages of yellow fever.

Fennel sailed to the head of the room to join Eelie and Garnel. All wore long leather boots, green biker shorts, emerald tiaras on which Garnel had insisted, and not much else except for chartreuse armbands that clashed with their shorts. Their appearance was made worse by their choice to go topless, but they had a point to make, as Eelie explained: "The tyranny of humans has forced me to mask my true self. The inner ME has been repressed. I refuse the domination of all who do not acknowledge my centrality to all fairies and how much they owe to me. Oh, fairies, we do what we do all for you, in ways that deserve your gratitude and that you should feel free to commemorate often."

Once again, Eelie was lulling the Quyre troops into catatonia, and, if Grant had known, he might have led his fairies and won the day right then. Alas, information is never where it should be when required, and great catastrophes in retrospect look like stupid inadvertence.

Eelie's speech finished, and no one knew how to react. Was applause appropriate? Luckily, no reaction was needed because, with great solemnity, Fennel, Eelie, and Garnel, sailing a few feet above the ground, moved in a medium-sized circle, perpendicular to the floor. Slowly, their wheel approached the hall entrance as the Quyre intoned a solemn chant, whose burden was:

"Give us, give us, give us the Rite after midnight
Won't somebody help us get more strength and more sway?
Give us, give us, give us some Toe after midnight
Help us till we've gained all power over the Fay."

Forest looked around at the crowd and expected everyone to burst out laughing. But everyone stood stony-faced. Forest had to admit that awful as the Quyre was, they had taken his recommendation seriously. Any group that used ABBA songs for its ceremonies could not be all bad.

He took advantage of the distraction caused by the Quyre to dart to the conveyor belt platform. He knelt and whispered, "Hey. What's your name?"

"Zach," said the distracted twentysomething, looking abject.

"Zach! That's right! You go to my gym."

"That's right."

"How are you liking it?"

Zach gave him a look that said, "This is not the time for this discussion."

Forest said, "You're right. We can talk about it later. But I'm so glad to see you."

"You were the last person I thought I would see here."

"I remember talking with you about being comfortable in my gym, especially around bathrooms. Do you remember?"

Zach nodded.

Forest continued, "What brought you here? How did you get mixed up with this?"

"I needed the money."

"I understand. But no money is worth being bullied by Fennel. I don't know if you trust me or not, though I hope you do."

"What difference would it make?"

Forest leaned over and murmured in his ear. Zach remained as still as an opera fan waiting for a high note. But Forest thought he detected a faint nod, and it was enough. Their whole dialogue had taken seconds, and Forest moved back unnoticed to the food tables.

Glancing at the front door as the Quyre continued to circle, Forest assumed Grant's men would charge in momentarily, but he had no idea what to expect. Mothra's kidnapping had kept Forest out of the loop about battle plans. The Quyre's militia had arranged themselves like toy soldiers at equal spacing throughout the hall, glass guns ready. Humans were on the ground, fairies, in the air. All faced the entrance to the hall, through which anyone who wanted to disrupt the Rite would have to pass. For extra security, the main door had been reinforced with iron and a thick deadbolt. Although in police procedurals that Forest loved to watch, it never took much to break down a door, this one was bolted as tight as a virgin.

Sharp knocks at the door, in what sounded like a pre-established rhythm, interrupted Fennel, Eelie, and Garnel in their ABBA wheel. From Grant's descriptions, Forest recognized Sandor, looking resplendent and wearing not much; Sandor looked to Fennel as if for instructions. Although everyone in the Quyre's army expected Fennel to lecture about the discourse of knocking, he just gave Sandor a nod, in a way that barely interrupted the drone. The Quyre guards reset their rifles as Sandor sailed to the door, drew back the deadbolt, and opened it on the dark hallway.

There, looking tired and pale, stood Ray, with Craigy slumped on his shoulder like a sack of sleepy potatoes. Forest, at the far back of the hall, could not see what was happening, but the Quyre trio altered the chant as Craigy entered and sang with ghoulish enthusiasm and dodgy intonation:

> "I'm eatin' toe
> I want the world to know
> That I'm eatin' toe
> I want the world to know
> That I'm eatin' toe...."

Forest, who was too far back in the hall to see what was happening, thought that abandoning ABBA was not a good sign, but knew that his opinion counted for nothing.

As for Ray, two members of the Quyre guard seized Craigy from Ray as soon as he came in and tossed Ray a substantial suitcase filled with bills. True to their bargain, the Quyre had made Ray rich. But at that moment, he did not look as if he cared about the money, though he did open the suitcase to check how much there was.

While Ray had whispered, "Careful—he's asleep," to the guard, they had either not heard or did not care, for they dumped Craigy roughly on the conveyor belt and strapped him to the bracket with twine. Doing so at last awoke the toddler, who, doing what he did best, began to scream his lungs out and howl, "Way! Way! Up!" He wriggled hard in the brackets, but they were bolted tight to the platform. On cue, Zach turned the conveyor belt on, and it began to revolve slowly with Craigy on it. Fennel, Eelie, and Garnel descended from their Ferris wheel to the floor and positioned themselves at equal distances around the platform. They licked their lips as Craigy, crying and writhing, went by. Fennel took from his shorts a small bolt cutter; Eelie clipped in false teeth that were sharp as daggers; Garnel had a wrench. They were ready for the feast.

Ray, feeling sick, watched as Craigy was strapped down and his socks removed. Although he still did not know exactly what the Quyre would do, the instruments that the three brandished were bad. He felt himself screaming, "This is wrong. Stop!" but no sound emerged. Desperate, he attempted to rush to the platform to free Craigy, but he was blocked by the Quyre guard, including Sandor. In their eyes, Ray was almost too easy an enemy for them, an annoyance but nothing more. Sandor and Grayson hustled him to the door. Ducking beneath their arms, he tried to wriggle past them and run—but every time, they snatched him back. He found himself airborne as the fairies pushed him to the exit. At the main door, Grayson lifted the deadbolt, while Sandor held Ray to throw him out.

THUMP. THUMP. THUMP.

Just as Ray was about to be sent out as unceremoniously as Craigy had been taken in, loud noises came from the windows at the other end of the room. The Quyre, knowing that the Paramount's windows were vulnerable to attack, had covered them with iron bars that prevented entrance or exit. Since the bars were plainly visible, they assumed that no one would bother attacking from the outside. But despite its seeming pointlessness, just such an attack was happening. Thud after thud came from outside, as if desperate zombies were hammering the room.

Careful not to interrupt the Rite, Fennel nodded to Sandor to open the curtains so that they could see what was happening. Outside, Grant's men were sailing directly into the windows and bouncing off the iron bars. It would have been a ridiculous sight, something like a Whack a Fairy game, if it had not been so serious. Everyone knew that Grant's men would never get into the hall through the windows because the Quyre had prepared too well for that possibility. Forest's heart sank each time Grant's men ricocheted off the window like billiard balls. It took the Quyre less than a second to digest what was happening, to decide that it was not a threat, and to continue the Rite despite the thumping. The Quyre guard, however, remained focused on the windows, just to make sure that their enemies would never get in. That was their mistake.

Just after Sandor and Grayson opened the front door to jettison Ray, a phalanx of Grant's fairies (all those not busy battering the windows) steamrolled into the room. In a flash, a glass-storm of splinters flew at the Quyre guard, who, busy looking at the window, had not seen Grant's men enter because their backs were turned. Although the guard soon realized their mistake and spun around fast, the surprise had been effective. Grant's men took out at least half of the Quyre guard at their first entrance, and the bodies slumped to the ground, covered with glass splinters. Grayson, terrified, retreated to the back of the hall. Though the Guard still outnumbered Grant's men, the window feint had gained Grant's side a short advantage.

After this initial moment, events in the hall, which had dragged during the Rite, went at hyper speed. So much happened so quickly that it was almost impossible to track, with the Quyre, the guards, the servers, Craigy, Grant's men, Ray, Forest, Grant, and the wretched Zach, looking more terrified than ever, all zooming in different directions.

Almost as one, the Quyre guard turned from the window and began firing toward the front of the room, aiming to hit Grant's phalanx down the middle.

Grant yelled, "Cardio chaos!" and his men went aloft. Cardio chaos was a move that they had practiced frequently with Forest in class, and they executed it perfectly. It involved deserting the phalanx formation to spread out in the hall so quickly that the Quyre guard did not know where to look. For those not in the battle, watching fairy sails outspread would have been a sight. The colors glittered and shone, and the sails whirred, flapped, twirled, and buzzed in a display like Chihuly on psychedelics. But no one in the hall could focus on the beauty.

The human servers realized that they had gotten into much more than they had bargained for and dove under the tables, trying to hide from the flying glass shards. Forest crawled under the tables as well, but soon felt that he was not helping anybody just by lurking. He darted back to Zach, still monitoring the conveyor belt to which the howling Craigy was tied. Zach, trembling with terror, seemed glad of Forest's company, although he was so petrified that it was hard to tell.

Ray, looking scared but unable to leave, slunk to the side of the hall and crouched against the wall, out of the way of the gunfire but able to see Craigy and what was happening to him. If there was any way to help Craigy without being killed, he would find it.

Grant, leading his men, had never looked stronger or more in control. He continued to yell out water-exercise-based commands: "Spinning right triangle! Cross-country spiral! Tuck jump cross in and out." Who would have thought that Forest's classes had been training in combat readiness? Even better, the commands baffled the Quyre guard, who had never seen fairies in such formations. Their faces wore the stunned looks of those encountering something impenetrable, like directions on IKEA furniture. As soon as Grant's men seemed to coalesce into one formation, they switched to a different one. The Quyre guard never got a clear shot because the second that they raised their guns to fire, their enemies were somewhere else. They tried to shoot anyway, and they covered the hall in shimmering bits of broken glass, as if thousands of champagne flutes had been shattered. But their aim was more enthusiastic than effective, even though bodies of the slain from both sides began to fall.

Fennel, Eelie, and Garnel, who were prepared for a disruption just like this, continued their chant in spite of surrounding chaos. By this point, the chant had changed to "Eat that toe-oh-oh" (to the tune of "Ring My Bell"). They patted Craigy's feet as he passed them on the conveyor belt, pinching and squeezing his toes while their eyes shone with glee. Craigy did his best to writhe and twist away from them, but they were too strong for him.

As Fennel dove down to Craigy, brandishing a bolt cutter to sever Craigy's right pinky toe, a strange high-pitched squeal came from below the conveyor belt platform, and the belt stopped moving. Craigy screamed louder than before, even as his voice grew hoarse. Fennel, eyes blazing, darted under the platform to blast the wretched Zach. He did not need to say anything because his fury was so apparent. But Forest was ready for Fennel and yelled out, "Oh, we definitely need more lube. The gears must have gotten dry."

"Keep the belt moving," screamed Fennel.

"Give me my cat," Forest screamed back.

"No," bellowed Fennel.

"Well, then get us more lube," Forest shrieked.

Fennel, cursing, nodded to Sandor to find something to help the track keep moving.

Forest was less frightened of Fennel than he was terrified that Mothra would be hurt with all the flying glass, even though he knew that her carrier was keeping her as safe as anyone in the hall. Just then, Grant, swooping low underneath the platform, seized Forest in his arms and sailed with him away from the central platform to the darker side of the hall, less in the way of broken glass and the occasional falling body.

"What are you doing? Put me down! There's glass everywhere," screamed Forest.

"But thou gavest me the signal, for which I have so long waited," said Grant.

"I what?" bellowed Forest, as Grant continued to sail with him.

As he and Grant sailed away, Forest saw Fennel glaring at him with all the malice of a confirmed catnapper. Presumably, Fennel knew that he and Grant were up to something. But he rejoined the chanting with Eelie and Garnel anyway, as if he were so confident that whatever Forest and Grant would plan, he would be more than equal to it. As Grant had warned Forest, once the Quyre had tasted toe, they would be invincible.

Forest, much as he disliked sailing, was happy to be back in Grant's arms. The days since Mothra's abduction had felt like weeks. As the hall continued in chaos, he and Grant were in a tight embrace, a little island of happiness amid darting bodies, multicolor sails, ritual chanting, wailing toddler, and explosions of glass.

Landing carefully in the corner, Grant murmured to Forest, "So thou'rt ready?"

Forest took a step back from their embrace. "Huh?"

As his answer, Grant drew near Forest, pulled his rear close, and let Forest feel how hard he was. "Now."

"You have a strange sense of timing. I need to help Zach."

"Did I not hear thee calling for more lube? Dost thou remember thy promise? And, if thou hast not noticed, Sandor is taking a more than friendly interest in Zach, so I think he'll be okay."

"Wait, but I was talking about—."

"When will there ever be a better time? I have gone day after day dreaming of thy body, of holding thee, of giving thee such pleasure that thou wilt remember it forever. The Quyre are out to kill both of us. Don't let them get to either of us without our having had this chance."

How could Grant possibly think that this was an appropriate moment? But then he remembered what he had said about lube to Grant, who had taken him literally.

But Mothra needed help!

But the Quyre were about to eat a child!

But a ferocious fairy battle was taking place everywhere around them!

But Grant took him in his arms and gave him a long, deep kiss. For Forest, it had been so long. Despite all the chaos, he could feel himself responding, knowing how much he wanted Grant. In spite of himself, it was impossible not to follow as they retreated deep in a corner and Grant's trousers slipped to the floor, followed soon by Forest's gym sweats.

The Rite seemed to have entered a new phase. Fennel, Eelie, and Garnel stopped their chanting and began to intone the prayer of the Rite: "O Lord of Fays, give me the strength to eat the toes I can, the patience to avoid the toes I cannot, and the wisdom to know the difference." The chant continued in a drone as they circled the screaming, barefoot Craigy.

The chaos in the room is best conveyed not through narrative but through a sample audio transcript:

"Plank jacks with single hands!"

"Quick: up to the left. No, down to the right. No, now they're zig-zagging. Try again. I think you got one of them!"

"Glass shards are all over the custard."

"WAAAAAAY!"

"Who are you calling a loser, fairy scum?"

"Tell me how badly you're wanting this cock, boy."

"Craigy, I'm coming as soon as I can!"

"Meow, meow, meow" (in a tone of faint distress).

"Fennel is gonna kill me, Fennel is gonna kill me, Fennel is gonna kill me."

"O Lord of the Fays...."

"Harder, Daddy! It feels so good!"

"When are we getting out of here? This was not what I signed up for."

"The toes are so perfect, so gorgeous, so ready."

"WAAAAAYYYY!"

"Eat glass, you Quyre sucker... damn, missed again."

"Where did Grant go? Why isn't he giving us the formations?"

"Oh yes! I'm gonna come, I'm gonna come!"

"... the wisdom to know the difference."

By this point, Grant was thrusting hard into Forest, who was thrusting back with his hips in a perfectly timed movement. It was the best sex either of them had ever had. For Grant, he had wanted Forest for so long that being with him at last felt like an answer to a long list of prayers. For Forest, it had been forever since he had felt an intimacy that made him want to be a good bottom, to hold and be held, and to grab Grant's amazing glutes and draw them toward him. He turned his head to kiss Grant again, ready for an orgasm that would end all orgasms.

And then—

"Forest? Is that you? It's Ray."

Awkward pause, accompanied by sounds of loud chaos from the rest of the hall.

"Ray?" said Forest, aghast. Even though Ray had entered earlier, Forest had been too far away and too distracted to see him. Another awkward pause. "What are you doing here? Are you working for the Quyre?"

"I'm rescuing Craigy. What are you doing here?"

Even more awkward pause, since the relative positions of Grant and Forest made it obvious what Forest was doing there.

Ray resumed, "I can't let them touch Craigy. Please, please help me."

"Ray, this is Grant. Grant, Ray is my ex."

They all looked at each other, took a beat, and then Grant and Forest clumsily pulled up their pants.

Grant was the first to speak. "We will not get to Craigy as long as the Quyre is in charge. They grow more powerful the closer they are to his toes. Although they still have more chanting to do, the first bite will bring each of them power that is almost unlimited. My advice is to wait until my men have neutralized the Quyre guard. Then we rush the table and rescue Craigy."

Suddenly, they all heard Fennel's voice, bellowing in loud, terrifying tones: "FREEZE."

CHAPTER 23

"FREEZE" HAD come from Fennel while he was bending down with his bolt cutter to cut off Craigy's big toe. It stopped everybody in the hall. The paralysis that the Quyre had formerly used only on Ray they now used on everybody. Fairy soldiers sailing in battle plopped onto the floor, and two or three soldiers hurt themselves on the glass splinters, though not seriously. Servers cowering under the tables had already frozen in fear and now were even more frozen. Craigy at last was hushed. Over the room fell a silence, as if someone had just announced the death of a major diva. Whereas seconds before the hullabaloo had masked even the orgasmic moans of Forest and Grant, now there was almost total silence, broken only by the mews of Mothra. (Evidently, she was exempt from Fennel's magic, which she considered only fair.)

In the near silence, Fennel strode to the corner where Grant and Forest had been going at it. He seized Forest, who in retrospect was grateful to Ray for giving him a chance to pull up his sweatpants, and neither Grant nor Ray could stop him. Fennel dragged him back to the center table with Craigy on the tracks and held his bolt cutter right next to a sensitive area of Forest's body. Gripping Forest with one hand, Eelie helped Fennel to grab Craigy's foot and move the bolt cutter. As he did so, he glared at Grant with a look that dared Grant to try to rescue Forest.

To his captive audience, Fennel said, "Thus starts the power of Fairy. And by power, I mean not governmental power that monopolizes state violence. I mean power that irradiates, spreads, infuses all walks of life through discourse, power that circulates ceaselessly, power that glows. Fairy power will be in the bread you eat, the water you drink, the thoughts you think, in the depths of your feelings. Fairy power will be inescapable, so pervasive that you will not know how it surrounds you like an atmosphere, envelops you in its all-encompassing web. My preparation for the Rite, for which I have worked night and day, has made me alone capable of understanding how fairy power works, compounding the recursive effects of agent and structure, and

AAAAAAAAAGGGGGHHHHHH." Fennel ended with a scream only slightly less intense than a bottom with insufficient lube.

A tiny tinkle of glass sounded, hardly audible.

Immediately, Fennel released both Forest and Craigy's foot and slumped awkwardly to the floor. Simultaneously, Eelie and Garnel crumpled like wet paper and lay still. The Quyre soldiers stared at each other, Grant's men stared at the Quyre guard, the servers stared at the platform, Mothra stared at nothing (as usual), and Craigy renewed his howling. Grant sailed up to Forest and held him in a tight embrace.

Ray alone did what needed to be done. He rushed to the platform and untied Craigy, who had begun to howl again. "Way! Up!" Craigy shouted and he soon was lifted off the platform. Ray swept him up over his shoulder and murmured to him, trying to settle him down. As he did so, the room filled with the buzz of conversation as the Quyre guard and Grant's men puzzled over what had happened. Sandor's voice was heard above the rest: "Look! Custard everywhere. What happened?" It was true. The area around the Quyre was coated in bloblets of too yellow custard.

Forest whispered to Grant, "I think my plan may have worked."

"Thy plan?"

"The Quyre asked me to bring a saffron custard. I made it in my old glass dish. When I got here, I realized that if I left it on one of the burners and turned the heat up, sooner or later it would explode. I positioned it so that most of the glass would fly toward this platform. It was a million to one shot that it would hit the Quyre, and, though I can't believe it, it looks like it worked. That's why there is custard everywhere. I may not get a Michelin star, but maybe killing three fairies at once counts as a home run. Thank God the Quyre received the brunt of the glass and not Craigy."

All anyone had heard was the tiniest tinkle, as if a demitasse cup had rattled a bit while coffee was poured. But that had been enough to wipe out the Quyre. Forest's exploding tray had sent glass shards everywhere at a frightening speed. The combination of glass and speed met all the ancient requirements for killing fairies, technically known as faticide. Fennel, Eelie, and Garnel were cut down in what they had planned to be their moment of triumph. Craigy, fully toed, was safe in Ray's arms, while, if Forest was seeing correctly, Ray was crying. Most of the servers fled as soon as possible. They did not even stop for their money. The wretched Zach seemed to have had some kind of episode underneath the platform; he lay in shock on the floor, eyes staring, mouth agape. Sandor was next to him and seemed to be trying to help.

Grant turned to Sandor. "Thou hast a choice. Thou and thy men canst surrender and support the Brownie Ban or thou canst die like the Quyre."

"Brownie Ban oppresses fairies," said Sandor.

"The Quyre oppressed fairies," said Grant. "But there's a choice between peace and limited power or war and absolute power."

Sandor looked at his men, who were gazing at their fellows dead on the ground and at the gruesome bodies of the Quyre, backs covered with glass shards. The energy drained from them.

"Does this mean we're not going to get the reward we were promised?" asked a sad voice from the crowd.

Sandor just glared.

A faint voice broke the silence: "Enough fighting."

Everyone looked to see where it came from. "Garnel!" yelled Sandor, rushing to his side. Evidently, the glass had not burrowed into him quite as hard as it had with Fennel and Eelie. Garnel was injured, hovering between life and death, but capable of speech: "I did not understand, when this started, just how much it would cost. For the others, it became an obsession." Garnel's usual stream of chatter continued, but his voice faded into inaudibility. Members of Sandor's guard rushed to his side to see if they might save him. Even JX and Tren joined in to help.

While the crowd huddled around Garnel, Grant sailed slowly to the center of the room and said, "Gentlemen, Fairy has a new hero." Forest marveled at how bravely all Grant's men had fought. They had risked their lives, and it was a miracle more of them had not been hurt. The Quyre guard had fared less well, but not for lack of courage. It seemed sad that they would not get their reward, though Forest did not know what it was. And Ray, of all people, had come to rescue Craigy! Forest could not believe it and pondered what that rescue must have taken. In his mind, Ray was the hero of the evening, second maybe only to Craigy, who had not deserved anything that had happened to him and, all things considered, had weathered it all like a trooper.

Grant continued, "Forest, when it looked as if all was over, thou led'st the good fairies to victory. Fairy will always be in your debt."

Loud cheers of "Forest! Forest!" followed.

"I have no idea what you are talking about," Forest said.

"No one except thee would have put the glass on the burner where it would explode. Even after Fennel froze us, thy idea rescued us all. Fairy pays you homage."

More cheering. Tren even showed emotion, and JX was crying as if Dorothy had at last made it home to Kansas.

Forest looked at Grant, baffled. "Yes, but I had no way of knowing that they would be directly in the line of fire when the explosion happened. That was just luck."

Grant answered, "Luck is part of being a hero."

Forest was sure he looked stupider than usual, unable to process what was happening.

"Thou art now protected by the power of Fairy," said Grant.

Uh-oh, Forest could not help thinking.

"How can we show our appreciation?"

Forest was so caught off guard that nothing came to his mouth. The room was silent as everyone waited for his answer. As Forest soon realized, the problem was that it was too silent.

"Where is Mothra?" asked Forest. He did not hear her mewing. When he looked to the corner where her carrier had been, nothing was there.

"MOTHRA!"

"Mothra?" muttered some of the fairy soldiers to each other.

"Is that his way of saying 'mother'?"

"Moth who?"

"Is a giant moth about to sail into the building?"

Ignoring them, Forest pushed his way to Garnel, still chattering inaudibly about nothing.

"Garnel!" Forest cried.

"I am so happy about those napkins. They really gave the feast just the boost it needed."

"Garnel!" Forest tried again.

"And then there was this lady on TV and she was showing everybody how to fold napkins correctly but she had just terrible hair and it looked almost blue in the light and I did practice a little of the folding with her just to make sure that I remembered and…."

"Garnel, where is Mothra?"

Garnel, looking puzzled, stopped his word salad and turned to Forest.

"What?"

"Mothra. The cat. Kidnapped by the Quyre to manipulate me."

"Hmmmm," said Garnel, looking puzzled. "Did we really do that? That must have been Fennel or Eelie. They are so smart."

"Garnel, where is Mothra?"

"Is Mothra the cat? I noticed some very hunky man who kept calling me 'dude' carrying her off. I just assumed he was her owner."

Garnel continued his usual stream of chatter, but Forest, eyes wide and desperate, turned to Grant. His lips formed the words, "Help me," but no sound came out.

Grant said to the assembly, "We are going to rescue Forest's cat, Mothra, who has been stolen by a man named Grayson. It's the least we can do, considering what Forest has done for us."

CHAPTER 24

ALTHOUGH FAIRIES in flight are invisible to non-fairy eyes, the watchcams of Pine Rapids, if they had been able to see the procession out of the Paramount early on that cold March 15, would have recorded a strange sight. At the head, Grant held Forest aloft. Forest, preoccupied with Mothra, was too stressed out to struggle and was urging Grant to sail faster and faster. Grant's men had taken the Quyre guard as not-quite-prisoners. A few dog-preferring fairies had grumbled at being made to search for a cat, but Grant had convinced them to get over themselves. They sailed in small clumps, with Grant's men behind each bunch of Quyre guards, ready to target any guard who might escape from the job at hand. Sandor personally held on to Zach, who was still recovering from the Rite.

Somehow, in the pressure of the departure, Ray and Craigy had been swept up in the action, even though both needed to be home in bed. "You two," Sandor had yelled, "go with him!" Sandor pointed to a particularly tall fairy, with long, sculpted arms. Ray had assumed that the fairy would guide him and Craigy back home, but, to his surprise, the fairy gathered them both in his arms and sailed along with the others, to look for Mothra. Ray clung desperately to Craigy, who was the happiest person in the procession: "Up! Up! Up! Twee! Building!" He laughed and laughed, which, given all he had just endured, seemed like a healthy response. Ray, for all his terror, could see that Craigy was having a wonderful time and that let him relax a tiny bit. He also worried about his briefcase full of cash, which he had left back in the Paramount. If he went back to get it, would anybody hold him responsible for the debacle?

Everyone landed more or less at the same time at Grayson's, a few blocks from Forest's gym. Forest and Grant rushed in first. In spite of himself, Forest was impressed by the size of the reception area, which was about six times the space of his own gym. There was a lounge area, a coffee bar, and even junk food machines with snobby snacks, such as a brand of expensive low-carb potato chips that Forest thought tasted like chalk. But all this went by in a flash. He yelled to the reception clerk, "Where is Grayson?" but she was so stunned by the appearance of the crowd that she stood there, speechless. Forest tried again: "Where is Grayson's office?" She pointed down a hallway.

But Grayson's office was locked and, even after searching the gym's aerial studio, the partycycling room, the dedicated joggling track (jogging and juggling at the same time), Piloxing, and much else, there was no sign of either Grayson or Mothra. Forest had now had a thorough tour of his competitor's gym and hate-toured every square foot. But none of that mattered next to the need to find Mothra.

He conferred with Grant. "Grayson knows that the Quyre can't protect him now. He must have taken Mothra for leverage. If our side had lost, where would your men have gone for protection?"

Grant considered. "We would need the help of someone with power and with the ability to resist, if not destroy, the Quyre."

"The only being I have met in all this time who had any resistance to the Quyre was Isaac."

Grant looked puzzled.

"The gnome, the Great Parking Lot Gnome."

Grant's eyes grew wide. "Thou'rt right! Grayson may have fled to beg the gnome for help. Let us go."

Grant ran through the halls of the gym and instructed all the fairies to reassemble in the reception area. Ray had taken Craigy to look at the treats on display in the coffee shop. Craigy wanted all of them, the shop was not yet open, and Ray soon came to regret his decision to distract Craigy with treats. He did buy him some sugar-free gummy worms from the vending machines, which made Craigy happy enough for the moment.

The fairies reassembled with new instructions from Grant. Ray asked Craigy, "Do you want to go up in the air again?"

"Up! Up!" Craigy responded. Forest, Grant, Ray, Craigy, and the fairies all rose once again away from Grayson's gym and toward the potholed parking lot, the den of the gnome who was also Isaac. With Grant's permission, Sandor took a second to make sure that Zach was okay. Zach reassured him that he was fine and would be able to get home. After taking Zach's number, Sandor hurried to join the rest.

As soon as they landed, Forest and Grant ran to the largest pothole and, with no hesitation, leaped into it despite the freezing water. At this, the others stared in horror. Grant's men, trusting him, were willing to jump, but the Quyre guard were suspicious:

"How do we know that the gnome is down there?"

"What if we can't get out?"

"Maybe the cat is just wandering around up here. Can we just check out the parking lot?"

Sandor, who had quickly caught up with them, was embarrassed at his men's cowardice: "What bunch are you! Time to fairy up and grow sails. Jump now." And with that, Sandor jumped with as much gusto as Grant and Forest before him.

Below, he saw Grant and Forest talking about how best to search for Mothra, though Forest was so agitated that he could not help screaming "Mothra" every fifteen seconds. As fairies landed, he and Grant sent them to look in the darkness surrounding the gnome's house. He and Grant would look in the house itself.

They tried the front door, which was locked. After Forest pounded so hard at the door that he thought he would break his knuckles, the door opened to a smiling Isaac saying, "I think I have something you arrre looking for."

"Mothra? Where is she?"

"No, not Mothrrrra. I should have said 'someone.'"

And Isaac walked them to the corner of the front parlor, where, hiding in a miserable heap, was none other than Grayson.

"You promised to hide me!" he yelled at Isaac.

"And I kept my prrrromise. I hid you when you asked me. You did not say for how long you wanted to be hidden."

Forest interrupted, "Where is Mothra? Where is my cat?"

Sneering, Grayson responded, "Dude, you're never getting that cat back. I opened the cage in the darkness outside. She could be anywhere, and no one will find her."

Forest rushed forward to beat the daylights out of Grayson, but Grant pulled him back. "Not worth it. Let's go outside and find Mothra. We'll take care of him later, where it hurts."

Forest strutted away in what used to be called high dudgeon to begin the search for Mothra in the darkness. As he passed Ray and Craigy (how had they gotten down here?), he could hear Ray muttering to Craigy, "We're going look for a cat, okay? Can you help us find the cat?"

Craigy answered, "Baaaaa!"

Ray responded, "I'm pretty sure it's the sheep who says 'baaaaa,' but that's a good start."

Forest, desperate to find Mothra, was stunned at Ray. This man had been so self-absorbed that he was like a sponge soaking up himself. He had been the worst, most egomaniacal partner that Forest had ever had. And here he was, comforting a small child and even doing a good job of it. For a second, he wondered if Ray's interest in Craigy was entirely kosher, but he hated himself for even having the thought. Too many generations of gay men had been yanked out of children's lives because of just such thinking. And the care and concern in Ray's eyes were so unfamiliar and so genuine that Forest was at a loss for words. How had Ray changed?

Ray, desperate to get home, was stunned at Forest. This was a man who had been so indecisive that he could hardly put on underwear in the morning. Forest had been the most overthinking, fussy, small-minded partner that Ray had ever had. And here he was, a hero to the fairies and commanding men as if he were used to it. For a second, he wondered if Forest's desperation to find Mothra was entirely kosher, but he hated himself for having the thought. Too many generations of gay men had depended on their pets for emotional support available nowhere else. And the care and concern in Forest's eyes were so unfamiliar and so genuine that Ray was at a loss for words. How had Forest changed?

Forest turned to the fairies. "As you've probably figured out, my cat's name is Mothra. According to Grayson, she's in here somewhere. Please do your best to find her."

"But it's now dark. How will we find the cat?" asked Sandor.

"Just use your phones," Forest snapped.

Mothra, like most cats, would be able to see where she was. But dark vision was harder for both humans and fairies. Everything had happened so quickly that Forest had not had a chance to develop a real plan, such as bringing a floodlight. "Just stay in sight of the gnome's house and you will be fine. I doubt that she's gone far. If it helps, she sometimes responds to the Mothra song from the movies, if you want to try that."

For what seemed like hours and hours but was in actuality only about thirty minutes, the fairies searched. The darkness echoed with the sound of Mothra's name and occasional wisps of the Mothra song. Everyone crawled on their hands and knees in the darkness, using their phones to illuminate the underground area. Only a few knew what Mothra really looked like, so the search was a guessing game. But to be fair, everyone gave it his best shot.

As the minutes passed, the sounds of Mothra's name gradually grew fainter. Forest could sense hope dying in the hearts of those looking. It was possible that Grayson had lied, that Mothra was somewhere else, and that this was all a waste of time. Mothra had been so close and Forest, furious at himself, had let her slip through his fingers. After all this, the Quyre was going to win where it mattered.

Just then, a small and faint "mow" came from the darkness. As Forest listened, he realized that the sound was not coming from Mothra. "Mow" again, in what sounded like an uncannily accurate human reproduction of cat speech. It did not sound like an adult trying to imitate a cat's speech, even though the speech was human. Instead, it sounded like what it was, a young child's imitation of a cat. At that age, overpracticing a tiny bunch of sounds has not yet wrecked the ability to imitate animal sounds. For adults, who know what animals are supposed to sound like, convention messes up the ability to reproduce animal sounds convincingly. For young children, however, imitating sounds is key, especially when learning to talk. As a result, Craigy could imitate a cat's meow exactly.

"Craigy! Do you see a cat?" yelled Ray.

"Way! Cat here!"

Dark as it was, Forest could see Ray, holding Craigy with one hand, make a blind scoop and catch something furry, though Forest could not tell whether it was cat, raccoon, or opossum. He could tell that it was meowing angrily, so Forest assumed it was a cat. And Forest would recognize that angry meow anywhere. Craigy and Ray had found Mothra. Forest was stunned, since Ray had just shown more concern for Mothra than he had for him in the entire time that they had been together.

Forest could feel a deep tension draining from his body now that he knew that Mothra was safe. Ray, weighed down by Craigy and the cat, trudged back to the light around the house, and he finally put Craigy down.

"You found her!" Forest answered, running back into the light, along with Grant. He would never have believed he would be so happy to see Ray again.

"I didn't find her," said Ray. "Craigy did."

Forest scooped up Mothra and held her close for a second, then knelt to Craigy: "Thank you so much for finding my cat."

"Mow," said Craigy.

Forest stood up, and Grant folded both him and Mothra in his arms, while Ray took Craigy's hand.

Ray and Forest then looked at each other.

"It's been quite a morning," said Forest.

"It has," answered Ray.

"What will happen to Craigy? Will he stay with you?"

Ray answered, "No. That's not fair to those who care about him. I will drop him off at his school, and they will handle the rest. Craigy has had a lot of adventure in the last two weeks and deserves a break. What about you?"

"I want to get Mothra back home safe. Tomorrow, I will go the gym and put my head together again."

Grant interjected, "Actually, Forest, there is a favor I must needs ask, on behalf of the fay." He whispered into Forest's ear.

"Can we talk about this at home?" asked Forest.

"Certes," said Grant.

Ray raised an eyebrow when he heard Grant's way of talking, but Forest just muttered, "Be like the British and put a wig on before you judge, as Michael Warner says."

Forest turned to Isaac, "Once again, thank you so much for your help."

Isaac answered, "I told you beforrrre what I wanted for you. Keep it moving."

Forest hugged Isaac and whispered, "Take today off if you need it."

"Neverrrr," Isaac whispered back. "The gym would collapse."

Forest was about to protest, but he knew that Isaac was right. And if Isaac wanted to come in to work, who was Forest to stop him?

As they were talking, the fairies in front of the gnome's house saw that Forest and Mothra had been united at last. They cheered and then, exhausted by the events of the last several hours, everyone realized that they had to get back home to their moisturizers and essential oils, lavender sheets and cappuccino. Getting everyone to jump out of the gnome's area back to the parking lot was easier than getting them down had been. Grant held Forest who held Mothra, and they all three made their way home, Mothra wriggling and squawking the entire time. Ray was Ubering back to the Paramount to collect his car and, as surreptitiously as possible, to get his cash, and then home to let Craigy watch cartoons and possibly get some sleep.

Forest needed some alone time with Mothra after Grant dropped him off at his apartment. He had never been so glad to see his drab furniture. Every fascia in his body had been worked to exhaustion. But before anything else, he made sure to get Mothra her Fancy Feast and filtered water and to give her a good brushing.

"My poor girl, I'm so happy to have you home." He continued to call her every pet name he could, to assure her that she was loved and to treasure knowing that she was safe again.

From somewhere, he heard a voice say, "Could we swap out that pate for some of the grilled food—the kind with the cheddar. It is so much better, and Fennel gave it to me every day." Forest froze and looked at Mothra. Her mouth was not moving. It's not as if she were actually speaking. But somehow, Forest knew her thoughts.

"You didn't think I'd spend all that time with the Quyre for nothing, did you? Let me tell you, there are things that we can improve around here. As it turns out, I have a list...."

Conclusion

Spectacular as the collapse of the Quyre had been, few in Pine Rapids knew what had happened. But FayTube could not get enough of Forest, Grant, Mothra, Craigy, and all that had happened. Forest happily participated in multiple interviews with FayTube commentators, although he was careful to omit a few details about what happened during the Rite. Fairies wanted to hear again and again how the Quyre had been defeated, and solemn warnings about the dangers of violating the Brownie Ban accompanied these retellings. For the time, at least, the fairies looked safe from a return of the Quyre.

The day after the Rite, Ray quietly returned Craigy to Kali Montessori. As the Quyre had promised, he did so with no detection, and no one ever came after Ray to ask about Craigy's disappearance. Craigy's teachers rejoiced to see that he was unharmed. If anything, he seemed to have thrived with Ray. But the situation at his home was not so good. Craigy's father had disappeared. Even though neighbors continued to care for Craigy, it looked as if the state would have to terminate parental rights, which meant that Craigy would end up in foster care. Ray followed every step of Craigy's journey and began looking into what it would mean for him to be a foster parent.

After the many imperfect efforts detailed in this narrative, Forest and Grant finally did have uninterrupted sex. It was so satisfying to both that the only smart thing was to repeat it as soon as possible, which they did. To them, it had felt as if the universe had been conspiring to keep them apart, and they celebrated the end of that conspiracy as often as possible. Zach and Sandor also turned out to have great chemistry and soon became a happy couple.

Grayson's gym ended up not having the success that might have been predicted for such a well-equipped gym. In part, the people of Pine Rapids were intimidated by its extravagance. It was so gorgeous that it felt wrong to touch the equipment. On top of that, things kept going wrong. Mics stopped working, dumbbell sets vanished, instructors had inexplicable car trouble at inopportune moments, equipment malfunctioned, weight racks collapsed. No one was ever hurt in these incidents, but after a few months Grayson's earned a reputation for being sketchy. No one could point to anything that happened regularly, but everyone had heard too many anecdotes about how, despite the membership fees, nothing at Grayson's ever worked the way it was supposed to.

Forest's gym, meanwhile, flourished. Its success was owing largely to the influx of fairy customers, who had never before had a gym where they could feel safe. Forest even acquired a large array of green towels just for them and continued to teach his morning water fitness classes, always attended enthusiastically by the fairy contingent.

Several weeks after the Rite, when the April moon was at its peak, one of the parks near Pine Rapids had an unexpected sound of pulsing music playing deep in the night. If you approached closer, you might have seen a ring of almost naked men, whose skin all gave the impression of being green, dancing to songs whose lyrics were in a language unknown to humans. As they danced, they stomped the ground with force so that they flattened the grass, plants, leaves, and anything else in their way. If you looked closely, you might have noticed that one dancer did not share the green hue of the others. He stood next to a handsome man who seemed to be acknowledged as leader. Near dawn, the leader asked that all the fairies in the circle bow to his non-green partner, as if to pay him some honor. Although most of their music was pop and disco, their last dance was a stately chaconne, called "Dance for the Green Men," which a seventeenth-century composer named Henry Purcell had written just for them.

In the morning, the men were gone. The only trace that remained was a circle of trampled grass, whose appearance mystified the park rangers.

The End

Keep reading for an excerpt from
Were-Geeks Save Wisconsin
by Kathy Lyons

CHAPTER 1

"I AM not going to wear that to a demon slaying." Nero Bramson stood naked to the waist in the Wisconsin snow. He was surrounded by his werewolf team, and they were headed into serious business. But apparently Pauly's brain was still on last night's Trivial Pursuit game.

"You lost, so you have to wear this," he said as he held up a pink tee. It read Crazy Cat Lady and was covered in stupidly cute kittens.

"We're here to do a job—"

"Yeah, yeah." His friend rolled his eyes as he waved toward the lake. "We're here to kill a basic demon who's been eating ice fishermen for who knows how long. Human body, big teeth. We can take care of one of those in our sleep." He shifted the tee in the predawn light enough to show off the glitter on the kitten collars. "You lost, you have to wear this today."

Nero bared his teeth, not surprised when it had no effect on his team. Pauly's partner, Mother, actually snorted as she started to strip out of her clothing. "You shouldn't bet on trivia when you suck at it."

"I grew up in Florida. What do I care about Big Ten football?" He'd lost the game—and the bet—on some obscure Michigan versus Ohio State statistic. "But I'm not going to wear something stupid and endanger this mission." He looked to the other two members of his team for help, but Cream and Coffee had already shifted into their animal forms. They were timber wolves and were prancing about in the snow, oblivious to Pauly's attempt to humiliate their leader.

"The fabric's so thin it'll rip in a stiff breeze," Pauly said. "It's not going to endanger anything."

Just his pride. Bad enough to wear pink, but the cat lady moniker was going to stick. And for a werewolf, that was adding insult to injury.

But Pauly was grinning as he tried to hide his cell phone, no doubt ready to snap pictures the moment Nero put on the garment. Mother was chuckling as she shucked the last of her clothing. And even Cream and Coffee had laid off rolling around in the snow to watch him with expectant expressions.

It was what he'd wanted for his team. They'd been going full-out for the past few months, and everyone was starting to feel the strain. They'd taken out a banshee, two sewer demons, and his personal favorite: a zombie wizard on a bad acid trip. When Pauly had suggested a night of trivia and shots, Nero had thought it was the perfect stress relief. Who knew the guy had an encyclopedia of sports facts in his brain? Or that they'd finally get a location on the demon chomping on unwary Wisconsinites next to Lake Wacka Wacka? That wasn't its real name, but it was all he could remember.

He fingered the garment. It really was paper thin, and though the pink would stand out against the snow, his team was the best. They'd have no trouble taking out the demon, even if it spotted them a few seconds early. Maybe he could manage to rip the shirt on one of the evergreens.

"Come on," Pauly wheedled. "A gentleman always honors his debts."

"Now you're just being rude." He was not a gentleman by any stretch of the imagination, but damn it, he'd fake it if it meant keeping those smiles on his team's faces. "Fine," he said as he pulled the shirt over his head. "But you're paying for breakfast." It was his favorite part of every mission—the celebratory meal afterward. He had the perfect pancake house in mind, and it would cost Pauly a pretty penny since they'd all be starving after a demon killing followed by a glorious romp through the snow.

"Totally worth it," Pauly said as he snapped pictures rapid-fire.

"Get into position," Nero grumbled, and then he stripped out of his pants.

Damn, it was cold. He waited until everyone had gone full furry to slam and lock the van door. He put the keys in a box hidden inside the driver's side wheel well, then gratefully sprouted fur as he turned into the big, bad wolf of all those childhood fairy tales. Only this wolf was going to kill a demon before breakfast.

All in all, today would be a great day… even if he was going to be staring at pictures of himself in a pink tee for a long time. It stretched tight across his wolf chest, and though he tried to rip it as he breathed deeply, the fabric strained but didn't tear.

Pauly's gray muzzle pulled wide in a wolfish grin, and even Mother yipped quietly in laughter. He growled to silence them, but that only made Cream and Coffee snort. Nero then let out a stern bark and everyone settled. It was time to get down to business.

After five years of working together—three with him as alpha—they knew his moves as well as he did. They peeled out in formation, ranging wide as they searched for the demon. Cream scented it first, but the stench soon enveloped them all—brine badly covered by Axe Body Spray. Gah. Even a human nose would notice that. They picked up speed, and Nero quickly forgot the embarrassment of his attire. They were all caught up in the chase.

They found the demon squatting behind some young evergreens near an iced-over lake. It looked to Nero like a maraschino cherry: all its colors were off. Sure, it was shaped like a normal human male, but the skin looked pinker than flesh, the hair had green undertones, and the eyes seemed flat and creepy. Like glass eyes because—according to the fairy who had put them onto this thing—the demon didn't use its eyes to see. Those empty baby blues were for appearance only, since its whole body pulsed with paranormal radar and its receptors were on its skin. The only part of it that seemed normal was the mouth, though it was too wide and the teeth were sharp.

He went in first. It was his right as alpha. Plus, it was just plain fun to get in the first swipe.

The creature was focused on the lake, probably waiting for careless ice fishers, since there were some winter cabins nearby. It had been chomping on them, as well as cross-country skiers, for at least a decade before it had caught the Paranormal Alliance's attention. Thanks to the internet and cell phone cameras, it was getting easier to find the silent munchers. And now that it had been located, Nero's strike team would end it forever.

Seeing that the others were in place, he bolted forward through the snow. God, he loved this part—the sheer joy of his body moving like black lightning through the white landscape. Something about his wolf body erased his human aches. Bum knee, stubbed toe, achy shoulder—it all disappeared when he was a wolf.

He took a wide arc around the creature's hiding place, then dashed in to hamstring it.

The thing was prepared. Whatever radar it had had alerted it to the danger, but it was hemmed in by evergreens and too slow to leap away. It was faster than a human but not than a werewolf, and Nero dodged the swipe with ease. Better yet, he timed it just right, swerving around, then ducking under the swing, taking a bite of demon calf.

Score! He ripped out a solid chunk of the demon's leg. He was grinning around demon flesh.

Then the taste hit. Gah. Brine. It tasted like shit, but he'd done his job. Blood spurted from the creature's leg. Like everything else about this thing, the color was off. Orangey-pink like shrimp. He darted away before he could get covered in the crap.

He spit the mouthful out as soon as he could, his momentum taking him well out of the reach of the demon's hands. Mother and Pauly went in second. She'd go for the throat or crotch—she was vicious that way. Pauly would take out the other leg. Then it would all be over and they could go for a real run in the woods.

He kept his tail high as a message that said, All's good. He was spinning around when the first gunshot rang out.

It was the demon. Clearly it had been in this world long enough to learn about firearms, and it was getting off rounds with a surprisingly steady hand, given that Mother and Pauly had done their jobs. Both its legs were torn to hell and back. Some of its crotch too.

That was the thing with demons. They could section off parts of their bodies like a starfish. Its entire lower half could be torn away, and the upper body would still work. Good thing they'd trained for this possibility.

Cream and Coffee were already on it. Cream would take out the gun arm; Coffee would go for the throat. Some demons had to be dismembered. Mother and Pauly were rounding the trees, cutting closer and obviously anxious to take the bastard down. Nero tensed, ready for his pass as soon as Cream and Coffee delivered their strikes.

Bingo! Coffee got it across the neck, and weird blood sprayed. Cream had the gun arm clamped between his teeth and was ripping it off the bastard's body, but the thing was way more dexterous than they expected. The demon managed to toss the gun from one hand to the other—while being dismembered—and got off a shot.

Cream yelped in pain and dropped the arm. He still tried to run, but his back leg was fucked-up, and he tumbled nose over tail. Coffee's momentum had already taken him past Cream, but that was okay because Nero had already started his pass. He'd forgo the demon in favor of pulling Cream's ass out of the way while Mother and Pauly followed up with the killing blows. But he couldn't carry Cream as a wolf. It was way easier to scoop up a lupine with human arms, though the wolf weighed a freaking ton. He needed to get the guy out of the line of fire long enough to dig out the bullet. It was much too dangerous to attempt a shift back to human with a bullet in the body. There were too many bad places for the metal to lodge.

Not many shifters could make the change while moving, but fighters didn't often have the luxury of a quiet place to shift. He had been a year into training with Wulf, Inc. when he'd perfected the moving shift. It was one of the reasons he'd become a team alpha so young. He did it now, slipping into an energy place before resolving into a human still on the run. He even knew how to time his balance so that he could keep running while scooping up Cream's back end. The wolf would then run on his front legs while Nero managed the back.

That was the plan, and it started with flawless precision. He went from running on all fours to a dissolving flow of energy. His awareness took in the stupid T-shirt he wore, the ground and the air, the pulse of the demon's radar, and something more. There was a buildup of power from the demon's head. Coffee hadn't fully decapitated the thing, and there was growing magic centered at the spine, right behind the jaw.

That couldn't be good, but in this state, he didn't have the ability to broadcast a warning. It happened so fast. He'd barely sensed the power when it detonated.

The bastard demon exploded in a fireball that could be seen from a satellite. Fortunately Nero didn't have a body to burn. He didn't even feel pain—just a surge that tried to disrupt his energetic state. It was a mental scramble for him to ride the wave without disintegrating, but he managed, and then he resolved himself into his human body. He needed to scream a warning to his team. He needed....

The smell hit first. Even in a human body, he relied on his sense of smell.

Burnt flesh and smoke.

His bare feet registered blistering heat next. It burned his soles, even as he kept running.

Vision came next, and he saw a landscape that was no longer a winter wonderland. He was running through the center of a blast zone, and when he bent to scoop up Cream, all he got was charcoal.

He couldn't breathe. Everything felt choked off, even as it burned through to the bottom of his lungs. And all he heard was absolute silence.

He stumbled, falling to his knees but unable to release the charred bones of his friend. He looked down, his hands tightened, and the fragments slid between his fingers. He turned, frantically searching for his teammates, someone to share the shock with, but all he could see was burnt bodies and the melted ice of the water.

He saw the demon then, and shit, how could that thing be still alive? Sure, there were demons that could shoot fireballs, but he'd never heard of one that could create an explosion on such a massive scale. But the evidence was clear, as was the pink blob of partially dismembered demon body. It was beside the lake, rolling to the edge before it fell in. It wasn't going to drown. It would sink to the depths of the lake, where it would reform into a smaller, simpler body. Nero wanted to chase it. He could dive into the water and tear it apart with his bare hands.

But he couldn't leave Cream.

Or Pauly. Or….

He scanned the area, identifying the bodies, not from anything recognizable but from their locations on the blackened ground. Cream at his feet, Pauly just a few feet away. Mother beside her partner. And Coffee farthest away but facing toward him, because he'd been running back to help.

Four bodies. And a half-mile radius of scorched earth.

He started to shake, and his knees blistered. The heat from the ground was intense, and he was naked except for the tee. He stripped out of it and put it under his feet as he stood. He'd have to walk back to the van, thankfully out of the kill zone. His phone was there too. For some reason he thought he could call for help. Maybe someone could do… something.

It took another moment of staring before he realized he didn't need his phone. He had someone to call on for help: a fairy prince who owed him a favor. He'd saved the guy's life in a bar fight, of all things. He'd been at the right place at the right time, and by fairy rules, that meant Bitterroot owed him. The bastard also owed Nero an explanation as to why he'd sent them after this demon without telling them the thing could blast fire.

Clutching his hands into fists, he called out Bitterroot's full name three times. The condescending prick appeared instantly, almost as if he'd been waiting. He was a short guy or a tall elf, standing about two foot four, with bright eyes and a collection of butterflies attached to his body. The fairy was a collector of sorts.

Bitterroot appeared wearing his usual smug expression, but his eyes widened in shock as he took in the surroundings, including the charred remains at their feet.

Nero didn't let him get his bearings. "Why didn't you tell me?" he demanded. "You didn't say it could blast fire."

"You didn't ask," Bitterroot rasped, his expression still shocked. "There are rules."

Fucking asshole fairies, always with an excuse. But it didn't matter. They needed to handle the problem now. "Can you fix this? Can you help me?"

Bitterroot shook his head slowly, his gaze landing with horror on the ash outline of Mother's body. "I can't—"

"You can." Nero swallowed, the solution sitting heavy in his mind. The brass at Wulf, Inc. didn't have a lot of rules. The main precept was "complete the mission and don't die." But there was another: Never negotiate with the fae. Wolves always lose. But Nero didn't care—he did it anyway. "Give me a mulligan."

The fairy's gaze snapped back to Nero's. "That's not an easy thing." He took a deep breath. "It's an expensive thing."

"You owe me. I saved your life."

"Which gives you one wish." The fae rubbed his hand over his face in a weirdly human gesture. "A mulligan is complicated." Then he waved at the center of the blast zone. "What would you do different? How could they survive that?"

Nero didn't have an answer. He'd been lucky to have been in an energy state when the boom hit, and he'd barely survived it. The others might not be able to ride the wave like he had, and Coffee was a traditional werewolf. He never fully dissolved into energy but sprouted his snout and tail in an excruciating agony that took time. Coffee definitely wouldn't survive, but Nero had faith in his team to figure it out.

"We wouldn't attack at all," he said. "We'd take time to plan—"

"Not possible. You still have to attack today." Then, before Nero could argue, Bitterroot held up his hand. "I don't make the rules."

Nero choked back his frustration. Much of his brain was still screaming in horror, but what focus he had found a solution. "Can you hold on to the mulligan? Let me use it when I'm ready."

Bitterroot frowned, and a single brilliant red butterfly set off from his arm to flutter in front of their faces. He caught it gently, speaking quietly to it in a language Nero didn't understand. The fairy waited a beat, then another, as if listening to an answer. In the end, he looked up at Nero. "I can hold it for seven-times-seven days, that's all. And you'll have to pay."

Forty-nine days to find an answer to an explosion that had taken out a mile of Wisconsin. "Deal." His team was worth whatever the cost. No question.

Bitterroot's expression hardened. "You'll serve me, Nero. A year of your life for every day that I hold the mulligan open."

Nero's breath caught. Fairyland was a place of nightmares. No mortal belonged there, and no one came back sane. "Deal," he repeated, his voice strong, though inside he shuddered at the magnitude of what he'd promised.

"Standard rules apply. You can't tell anyone about this, and you can't go bargaining with another fairy to change this one."

Nero nodded. That part he'd already known. "Agreed."

"Agreed." Then Bitterroot stuffed that bright red butterfly in his mouth and swallowed it whole. He grimaced at the taste as he glared daggers at Nero. "Don't ever make me do that again."

Then he disappeared.

It was done. When he was ready, he'd call on Bitterroot and be zipped back in time to fifteen minutes ago—before the blast, before they even attacked. He'd be able to redo everything, making sure everyone survived.

But how?

He didn't have time to figure it out now. Police sirens were wailing in the distance, and he needed to come up with a cover story before they got here. The good news was that whatever he said wouldn't ultimately matter. Eventually he'd go back in time and fix the problem before it started.

In fact, he realized, everything he did for the next forty-nine days didn't matter. So long as he figured out how to defeat that fire blast, everything would reset once he used the mulligan. His team would survive, and life would go on as if this never happened. For them, at least. For him, he'd have to pay Bitterroot back. Which meant he'd be in Fairyland trying to hold on to his sanity, but that was a small price to pay for their lives.

SCAN THE QR CODE BELOW TO ORDER!

ANDY ELFENBEIN has edited Oscar Wilde's *Picture of Dorian Gray* and Bram Stoker's *Dracula* and written four academic books (some have even won awards). A graduate of Yale, he lives in Minnesota with his husband and a moderately demanding feline named Charlotte. When not teaching, he is an enthusiastic cook, a fitness instructor, a singer, and a dancer whose complete lack of talent has never stopped him. You can learn more about him and about the fairies of Pine Rapids at andrewelfenbein.substack.com.